Just as I was about to get up, I heard a terrible crashing noise at the back of the cathedral. Then a woman's scream and the high-pitched sound of breaking glass pierced the air. Perhaps someone had thrown a rock at one of the windows, I thought. Suddenly the ground shook under me, and I slapped my palms to the floor, trying to steady myself. From the altar, four people came running toward me.

"Run, boy," somebody shouted. "It's a quake. Get somewhere safe."

Blues across the Bay

WHITNEY STEWART

FOUR CORNERS PUBLISHING CO.
NEW YORK

Four Corners Publishing Company
45 West 10th Street, Suite 4J
New York, NY 10011

Printed in U.S.A.
Map © 2001 Mapping Solutions, Anchorage, AK.
Cover illustration by Bill Farnsworth.
Design by Kris Waldherr Art and Words.

05 04 03 02 01   5 4 3 2 1

Cataloging-in-Publication
(Provided by Quality Books, Inc.)

Stewart, Whitney, 1959-
Blues across the Bay / Whitney Stewart.–1st ed.
p. cm. – (Going to: San Francisco)
SUMMARY: Eric Wieman is a teenager from a small town in Massachusetts. A talented self-taught guitar player, his dream is to find a professional teacher and mentor, which he hopes to do at a summer music camp in San Francisco. He is also looking forward to seeing a friend from New Orleans, Lashley Moran, who will be at the camp. As Eric discovers that the world of music is much wider than he had imagined, Lashley seems to turn on him. Will music give the friends a second chance or force them apart forever? Includes a kid's-eye-view guide to real San Francisco sites and a companion map.
Audience: Ages 9–13.
ISBN 1-893577-08-2

1. Friendship–Juvenile fiction. 2. Guitarists–Juvenile fiction. 3. San Francisco (Calif.)–Juvenile fiction. [1. Friendship–Fiction. 2. Guitarists–Fiction. 3. Coming of age–Fiction. 4. San Francisco (Calif.)–Fiction.] I. Title. II. Series: Going to series

PZ7.S853Bl 2001 [Fic]
QBI01-700865

To Hans and Christoph, who keep me in melody;

And to Bubba–

May you be safe and in song.

ACKNOWLEDGMENTS

Many thanks go to my close friend, landscape designer Lillian Montalvo, who marched all over San Francisco with me. Once again, my husband, Hans Andersson, can be credited for helping me out of plot holes, and my son, Christoph, for his enthusiasm and his new interest in Alcatraz. I thank my niece, Andrea Andersson, who offered inspiration and a mattress–and Nora Burnett, Ashley Levy, and Daisy Uffelman, who received me kindly. Jolene Babyak, author of several books on Alcatraz, pointed out references. Matt Berman steered me in San Francisco. Music teachers Perrin Isaac, Diann Gardner, and Richard Harrison inspired textual riffs. And Michael Millard and Andy Mueller welcomed Hans and me to the Froggy Bottom guitar-making studio in Vermont.

Liselotte Andersson, John and Marsha Biguenet, Cindy Dike, Lampton and Elizabeth Enochs, the Fowler family, the Hilzim-Davidson family, the Martin family, Debbie Randolph, Chelle and Justin Rudelson, Coleen Salley, Ellis and John Scherer, the Schulingcamp family, Jill Silverman, all of my parents, and the fabulous Mayer family five made up a team of supporters for which I am ever grateful. As before, my publisher, Ruth Lutnick, and my editor, Susannah Driver-Barstow, gave me their enthusiasm.

AUTHOR'S NOTE

The characters in this novel are fictional. However, the prison experiences described are based on primary and secondary source material on prisoner life in Alcatraz prison. The Quickfinger Guitar Camp is invented, but an international hostel for travelers does exist at Fort Mason, as does the Blue Bear School of American Music. See **www.fortmason.org** for more information.

CONTENTS

CHAPTER ONE

Amongst Trees

Summer music camp. Thousands of miles from home. On the opposite coast of America. I was nervous and excited because I didn't know what to expect. All I could think about was finding a teacher who could help me play guitar like my favorite musicians: Muddy Waters, Jimi Hendrix, Carlos Santana, Eric Clapton, and Martin Simpson. I had listened to their music at my uncle's house since I was five, but I was a long way off from playing like them. I needed a teacher.

For the whole plane ride I tapped my fingers on my knees, listened to bad pop music through the airline's damaged headphones, and chewed bubble gum until my jaw was sore. Lunch was funky–the chicken sandwich was almost frozen in the middle, and the chocolate chip cookies and corn chips made me queasy. And I couldn't even look out the window because the guy next to me in the window seat had pulled down the shade and leaned against it to sleep. For the whole trip! I missed seeing the Rocky Mountains and the Pacific Ocean.

But I made it. And I found the camp van waiting for me near the taxis. "Quickfinger Guitar Camp" was painted on both sides of the van, and guitars and hands were painted all around. I waved at the driver, and he hopped out of the van to greet me and to take my backpack and heave it into the back. I picked up my guitar case and gingerly placed it next to my backpack. I didn't want the driver to mess with my instrument.

I was the only kid in the van, and the driver didn't say much beyond, "Have a good flight?"

"Sort of," I answered.

The driver shrugged and turned up his radio. "Good music!" he said as we drove off, and that was about it from him. I wondered if he was one of the instructors.

I calmed down on the ride in from the airport. Groves of trees caught my attention and became my markers for safety. Something about the straight and scrappy palm trees to the right of the road and the tall and ragged cedars to the left bolstered my spirits. I must have inherited this tree-marker thing from my Grandpa John, who lives deep in a forest in Vermont. He refuses to go anyplace if it doesn't have trees.

"Too much cement," he says of cities. My mom is the same way.

When I got out of the van at Fort Mason—where my camp was located—and wandered around, watching all the other kids, all I wanted to do was stand by myself at the edge of the highlands behind the camp hostel and stare out at San Francisco Bay. That's the Pacific Ocean out there, I thought as I sniffed sea air. I wished that Grandpa John could have been standing there with me.

A low, cottony fog blanketed the bay water and hid all but the top of the Golden Gate Bridge. Alcatraz and Angel Islands were out there somewhere, I thought, but I couldn't see them. The fog felt like my insides–dense, gray, and undefined. Standing there, stiff from the long flight, I was wishing my friend Lashley Moran would hurry up. I needed to see a familiar face. Sighing, I turned back toward the camp hostel. Forcing myself to walk away from the still cliff top, I imagined Lashley smiling and bouncing onstage with her guitar.

Like the other campers, I put my backpack and sleeping bag in my dormitory room and my guitar in my assigned instrument locker before joining the picnic line on the front lawn. Watching all the other camp kids greet each other by name and throw Frisbees and foam footballs, I wanted to join in. But I wasn't quite ready to introduce myself. I was still adjusting to the newness of everything. Instead, I sat down on an empty patch of grass to eat my second lunch, and I kept my eyes on the entrance to the grounds. I wondered if Lashley had changed since I had last seen her. Would she remember what I looked like?

Finally, I saw an old, blue Saab rumble through the camp gates. The Morans had driven all the way from their home in New Orleans to San Francisco.

Lashley and I had first met each other when I was in New Orleans the previous winter. That was my first trip out of New England, and I had gone to compete in the Quickfinger Guitar Contest. I had stayed with a boy named Ben Woo, and he had introduced me to his best friend–Lashley–who lives in a mansion. And I mean a mansion. I'd never before been inside such a place. At first I didn't want to get to know Lashley because she was competing in the same contest, and she had a much better guitar than I did. On top of that, her dad owns a recording studio, so she already makes her own CDs and knows all sorts of famous musicians.

But slowly I got over all that. She was rich. I wasn't. So what? She had a cool guitar, and I didn't. Too bad. We ended up as great friends anyway. I wouldn't have wanted to go to camp in California if Lashley hadn't agreed to go too. She was used to traveling all over the world with her parents, and I knew she'd know what to do if we both hated camp.

"It's about time, Lash," I shouted as she got out of the car. I sprang up from the grass, wiped my mouth, and sprinted over to her.

Lashley looked up and gave me one of her great smiles. Her reddish-gold hair hung loosely over her face, half covering her rounded blue eyes and freckled cheeks.

"Hey, Eric, you didn't have to drive across Texas to get here!" Lashley said before giving me a hug. "So what are you whining about?"

She let go of me and looked all around at the camp buildings. "Cool place. How are the other kids?"

"I don't know yet," I said, embarrassed that I hadn't talked to anyone. "I was afraid you weren't coming."

"Not coming?" Lashley grabbed my arm and shook it. "I just called you three days ago. You knew I was coming. We drove as fast as this blue heap will go. Some of it was amazing–like the Painted Desert–but crossing Texas took forever."

Mr. Moran cleared his throat loudly, interrupting Lashley. "Lash, the chair, please. Mom wants to get out. Hi, Eric. Nice to see you."

"Oh, sorry, Dad. Can you help me with the chair, Eric?"

Lashley opened the trunk, and I helped her pull out a folded wheelchair.

"Nice to see you too," I said to Lashley's dad as we opened up the wheelchair.

"Hi, Eric!" Mrs. Moran's singsong voice came from the front seat. "How's it going?"

Lashley and I pushed the wheelchair to the front passenger door of the car. Mrs. Moran's soft, smooth face broke into a huge grin when she saw me.

"Eric, come here and give me a hug. We've missed you!" Mrs. Moran hollered.

I leaned into the car and hugged her around the shoulders.

"This is so exciting–that you and Lash will be here together," she said.

Lashley held the wheelchair steady as her mother pulled on my shoulders to yank herself up. The lower half of her body is paralyzed, but her arms are thick and strong from physical therapy.

"One, two, three," she said, lifting herself. And she planted her bottom perfectly into the wheelchair.

"You okay there?" asked Mr. Moran, as he pulled a huge backpack from the trunk.

"We got it, sweets," Mrs. Moran said to her husband. "Nice to have a young man around again."

Mr. Moran brought the backpack to where Lashley and I were standing and shook my hand. "Hey. Are you calling me old?" he loudly asked his wife, trying to sound indignant. His face was contorted with disbelief.

From her wheelchair, Mrs. Moran shrieked with laughter. "Don't worry. You've still got a few more years!"

Mr. Moran rolled his eyes and exhaled. "Sheesh!" he said to me. "D'ya hear that, Eric? They want to put me out to pasture."

Lashley gave her dad a quick glance, squinting, and then she pushed her mother out and away from the car toward the camp lawn.

Mr. Moran watched as Lashley walked away.

"Good thing Mrs. Moran and I are going on this retreat in the mountains," he said to me, slumping his shoulders and bending forward at the waist. "We could use some fresh air and rejuvenation!"

CHAPTER TWO

Fort Mason

Fort Mason was absolutely the coolest place to go to camp. It is a collection of buildings spread out from a marina up to the headland, and it hosts creative activities of all kinds–playwriting, printmaking, folk dancing, yoga, t'ai chi, paper-making, psychic healing, and more. The campus is broad and often full of people, and the Quickfinger Guitar Camp used several buildings up on the high point. We were housed in a hostel that has several dormitory rooms, a quiet living room with a fireplace, and a cafeteria with a large dining room. At mealtimes, we could look out the huge picture window in the dining room and see a small, dark forest. I grew to love that view.

After saying good-bye to Lashley's parents on our first day, Lashley and I went for a walk around Fort Mason. We were supposed to check in with our guitar instructor in the late afternoon, but we had time to kill before the meeting. I showed her the lookout point behind the hostel where the shadows under the tall trees made me feel lost for a moment in an unfamiliar space. Seagulls and crows screeched and cawed above the trees, and the scent of seawater and fish drew me to the edge of the cliff to look out again over the bay. The fog had lifted, and I could now see boats on the water.

While I stood gazing at the bay, Lashley wandered behind me looking for crow feathers, which she had started collecting on her drive to California. Not finding any, she climbed up on an old cannon–left from the days when a military fort stood on the point–stretched her arms out wide, and shouted into the wind.

"Hurray for California! Hurray for seagulls and sailboats!" Lashley shook her loose hair in the wind. "Hurray for being out of the car!"

"Okay, lunatic," I said, rolling my eyes. "What do you say we go down to that long pier and see what kind of fish people are catching?"

I pointed down to the busy Municipal Pier that protected the west side of San Francisco's Aquatic Park.

"Okay," Lashley said as she walked back and forth along the cannon. "I'll follow you to the end of the world, Eric, my boy!"

"Yeah, yeah, yeah," I said. "How about just down to the pier."

Lashley slapped the back of her hand against her forehead in mock despair. "Oh, Eric. Do you doubt my loyalty and devotion to you?"

She almost slipped off the cannon as she closed her eyes and tossed her head back again. Her arms out straight in front of her, Lashley pretended to be walking blindfolded down the length of the cannon.

"Oops!" she shouted, suddenly jumping to the ground. She tumbled and landed on her rear, laughing. I walked over to her with my arm extended, and she grabbed my hand and pulled herself up.

"Ouch," she said, rubbing her backside.

"You're cracked," I said, smiling.

Lashley stuck out her tongue and wagged it from side to side. "Thanks . . . for the compliment."

I grabbed her elbow and led her toward the path down. "To the pier," I said.

As we walked down a steep and narrow staircase from Fort Mason to the pier, I looked to my left and watched four people on in-line skates tearing down an equally steep road that opened onto the bottom of Van Ness Avenue. One girl was shouting and trying to use the rubber brake on the back of her left skate. A tall boy was shouting out suggestions to the frightened girl, but she was losing control. Two others behind, screaming and laughing wildly, were about to run into the front pair. Seeing this screaming gang zooming uncontrollably down the road, a sweaty jogger below stopped suddenly, put out her hand toward the car behind her, and halted traffic until the skaters could make a quick left turn onto the pier.

"Hey, thanks!" yelled one of the skaters to the jogger. "I thought we were done for."

The jogger waved and then let the annoyed drivers continue on their way. One driver honked angrily at the jogger, but she paid no attention and started running again.

"That was close," I said to Lashley as we reached the bottom of the Fort Mason steps. "In-line skating, California style!"

"Yikes," Lashley said. She turned toward the Municipal Pier, and we started walking down the center of a road that was closed off to cars. "I'd never try that."

"Me either."

We were quiet for a few minutes, wandering past Asian American men and women who had positioned fishing rods against the stone wall of the pier. They were shouting to each other in a language I'd never heard, and watching their rods. As we walked toward the end of the pier, we passed two women who held their palms together at their chests and muttered to themselves.

"I wonder what they're saying," I said to Lashley.

Lashley had been looking out at the bay. "Who?" she asked, twisting to look around.

"Those women. They're muttering out loud."

"Prayers, I guess," she said, looking dreamily out at the water.

"Prayers?"

Saying prayers aloud and outside in public was something I'd never seen. My family certainly never prayed in public, except in church.

"How can you tell they're praying?"

Lashley screwed up her brow and looked at me, her head cocked to one side. "How can I tell? I don't know. I've just seen Asian people pray as they walk, I guess. They do it all the time in Thailand and Hong Kong."

"Huh," I said. "I wouldn't know." A twinge of envy tweaked me inside. Lashley didn't seem to realize that most kids didn't travel the way she did. I didn't think she knew many poor people.

Lashley shrugged, and we kept walking.

Reaching the end of the pier, we sat down on a cement bench and watched the activity on the water. The sky was now a deep blue behind bright, streaky clouds. The full white sails of three yachts swiped across the sky wall like paintbrushes across canvas. Pelicans and seagulls flew over us, and muscular men and women passed by in sea kayaks, heaving their legs and arms with every stroke. With my eyes, I followed the route of a ferry on its way out to Alcatraz Island. Lashley was quiet, apparently mesmerized by something in the bay.

"So, what do you think life was really like in that prison on Alcatraz?" I suddenly asked.

My dad and I had been watching Alcatraz movies together before I left for San Francisco. When Dad was a kid, he wrote a school paper on famous gangsters, and he had dug it out of a trunk for me to read. It had gotten me interested in criminals and Alcatraz. As far as I can remember, those are the only two subjects that have ever interested Dad and me both. I had told him I'd go out to Alcatraz for him and get some postcards.

"So what do you think?" I asked Lashley again.

She didn't answer. She was staring into space. I'm not sure she even heard me.

"Lash?"

No answer.

"Lash?"

No answer.

"Earth to Lashley!" I said loudly.

"What?" she said sharply, shaking her head and looking at me blankly.

"Where were you?"

She looked down. "Nowhere. Just thinking."

"About what?"

"Nothing." She glanced back at the water.

"You couldn't have been thinking of nothing. You didn't even hear me ask you a question."

She looked at her knees, not at me. "What did you ask me?"

I hesitated before asking her again. "Are you okay?"

"Yeah. Why?" Her face suddenly turned to stone.

"What's the matter? You seem kind of out of it."

"Nothing . . . well, maybe I'm tired after all that driving." Her eyes shifted away again.

"Huh," I said, looking away from her.

"So. What did you ask me?"

We both stared out at the bay.

I sighed, feeling a strange awkwardness between us that I had never felt before. I decided to ignore it.

"I asked you what you thought life had been like out in Alcatraz prison."

"I have no idea," she said. "I don't know anything about Alcatraz. It doesn't look very inviting."

We both strained to see the dilapidated white buildings on the rocky island.

"I'll bet it gets really windy and bitter cold out there," I said.

The idea sent an involuntary shiver through me. I zipped up my navy blue fleece vest.

"My dad told me that Alcatraz prison was meant for the worst criminals in America. Famous gangsters like Al Capone and Machine Gun Kelly did time out there."

"If I had lived in San Francisco back then," Lashley said, "I would have been afraid that one of the prisoners would escape and come into town."

"Yeah, but nobody can survive the swim from out there," I said. "The water is icy, and the currents can drag even strong men under."

"It doesn't look like a hard swim," Lashley said.

"Did you ever see *Escape from Alcatraz*, that Clint Eastwood movie?" I asked.

"No, and if it's scary, I don't want to see it. I hate scary movies."

"It's not scary. It's about three prisoners who dug holes in their cell walls, climbed up through a ventilation shaft to the cell house roof, and made their way down to the shore. Before they left, they put dummy heads in their beds so the guards wouldn't notice them missing. They made a raft out of stolen raincoats and were never seen again."

"Is it a true story?"

"It's based on one."

"You mean they got away? You just said nobody could survive the swim."

"Nobody knows if they got away. Most people believe they all drowned, but I wonder if they made it to the other side."

"Didn't the police search for them?"

"Sure they did," I said. "They launched the biggest manhunt of the decade. It would have taken a miracle for those guys to get away."

"Miracles shouldn't be wasted on criminals," Lashley said firmly. Her tone of voice caught me off guard again, but I let it go.

"I definitely want to go out to Alcatraz," I said. "What about you?"

"After what you just told me–NO. It sounds creepy."

I thought about this for a second.

"It may be creepy, but I am definitely going. My dad wants me to bring him back some postcards. Sometimes you can even meet a former inmate out there."

"I don't want to meet a former inmate," Lashley said. "How do you know if he is truly rehabilitated?"

"Maybe you don't," I answered quickly. "But the museum people wouldn't let a dangerous criminal speak to tourists."

Lashley was silent for a second. Shaking her head slowly, she said, "Lots of criminals go right back to crime, you know."

"Yeah, I know." I paused to think for a second. "But, you never know what someone could do with a second chance."

CHAPTER THREE

Jason's Resonator

After hanging out at the pier for a long time, Lashley asked a woman what time it was. The woman didn't seem to speak English, so Lashley pointed to the woman's watch. She showed us the time, and I groaned. We had only ten minutes to get back to camp to meet our instructor.

Racing back along the pier and up the steep cement stairs to Fort Mason, I could hardly keep up with Lashley. She and her fast legs, I thought. At the top, she turned to wait for me, and I panted heavily, the crisp air stabbing my throat.

When we finally grabbed our guitars from our lockers and went flying through the camp office door, breathless and red faced, all of the staff members stopped what they were doing and looked up at us. A severe, gray-haired woman frowned, and a muscular Asian American man stood up behind his desk and chuckled.

"Ah. Right on time," the man said, extending his hand to Lashley. His voice was soft and calm. "You must be Lashley Moran and Eric Wieman."

Lashley shook the man's hand. "Yup. That's us."

I was still gulping deeply for air and could not talk.

"I'm your instructor, Jason Parker," the man said.

I noticed he had a long braid of dark brown hair down the middle of his back. His strong shoulders pulled his chest up and out to the sides, very erect. He wore a clean, white T-shirt, which was tight across his torso, and new-looking blue jeans.

Most of the camp staff members went right back to work after Mr. Parker greeted us. But the gray-haired woman tapped her pen furiously against her heavy metal desk and stared at me with squinted eyes. Her hair was pulled back tightly in a bun, making her face look strained and mean.

"Uh . . ." I looked at Mr. Parker.

He let go of Lashley's hand and reached for mine. His grip was firm but not overpowering.

"Nice to meet you," I said softly.

I looked down at Mr. Parker's desk and spotted our camp applications and the photos that Lashley and I had sent in with our registrations. The gray-haired woman was still staring at us and sighing noisily. She finally looked away in exasperation, but I could tell from her slightly turned head that she was listening to us.

"Let's move into my music room, shall we?" Mr. Parker said, glancing at the gray-haired woman. "We'll be about an hour, Rosa," he said to her. She nodded in reply but did not look up.

Lashley and I followed Mr. Parker into the music building and down a long corridor of closed doors. I could hear music coming from the rooms, but the sounds were muffled.

Looking at Mr. Parker as we walked, Lashley asked abruptly, "Mr. Parker, why did that woman look so annoyed with us? Because we came in so loudly?"

Mr. Parker raised his eyebrows and looked into Lashley's face. "Yes, well, that's a good question," he said, sighing. "A very good question." He paused for a second as if measuring his words. "All I can say is don't let it bother you. Mrs. Alvarez is an unhappy woman. She is always looking for someone she can blame for her misery. This week it happens to be me."

"Oh" was all that Lashley replied.

"What did you do to make her so unhappy?" I asked without thinking.

Jason tilted his head and puffed a short burst of air through his nose. "Let's just say she has a problem trusting people she doesn't know. And I'm new here."

I wondered what Mr. Parker really meant. Why didn't Mrs. Alvarez trust people? I didn't dare ask.

We continued down the hall, passing a few other camp kids outside the music rooms. We all eyed each other carefully, but said nothing.

Mr. Parker stopped at a door with the word *Broadway* painted on it in red. I noticed that the other doors had only single letters on them: A, C, D, . . . and no words. Mr. Parker pulled out a set of keys from his pocket and unlocked and opened the door.

"Here we are," Mr. Parker said, holding the door open for us. "You two can take a seat." Lashley and I stepped inside, and Mr. Parker followed us. "Sorry, the folding chairs aren't very comfortable, but they keep you from falling asleep when you should be practicing."

We all sat down on the metal chairs, and Mr. Parker spread out his files on the desk. "First things first," he said, flattening out the sheets of paper in front of him, and then looking up at us. "I would like you to call me Jason."

Lashley and I nodded at the same time. "Okay," Lashley said. I mumbled in agreement.

"Mr. Parker just sounds too formal."

"Yeah, great," said Lashley. She seemed eager to be agreeable.

Jason read over our registration forms and made funny facial expressions, blowing out his cheeks, as he concentrated. I looked around the room at the amplifiers and the effects boards and hummed. Lashley watched her feet tapping on the linoleum floor.

"So." Jason looked up at us. His soft eyes and full lips opened into a wide smile. "I can see you both are very talented. The Quickfinger Guitar Contest is tough. You have been up against the best young guitar players in the country."

I felt a warm rush of pride give way and turn my face red.

"Now, how serious are you both about becoming professional musicians?" Jason asked.

I started to nod.

"Don't answer that without thinking," Jason cautioned. "Do you know what a musician's life is like? Ask yourself honestly before you answer. You're not here to flatter me, nor I you."

Lashley and I looked at each other, slightly baffled. I had never thought I would be anything other than a musician. Lashley, on the other hand, has many talents. Besides being a state champion in track, she loves to read. She and Ben Woo spend hours in bookstores arguing over which books to buy and swap. Suddenly it dawned on me that maybe Lashley didn't care about being a professional guitar player.

I answered first. "Well, I started playing with toy guitars when I was a baby. Then when I was six my uncle gave me a real electric guitar, and I started taking lessons. From that time on, I have never thought I would be anything but a guitar player. I am not even sure what else I could do."

"Okay," said Jason, nodding. "Fair enough. This summer you will get a better idea about the music profession."

"Okay," I agreed, slightly nervous about being with professionals.

Jason looked at me with stillness in his face. "I am not trying to persuade you to be a professional musician. I am just trying to get to know you. If we start together on the same path, we'll understand each other better and become a better team."

"Okay," I said, beginning to feel comfortable with Jason.

He looked at Lashley now. "And what about you?"

Lashley looked uncharacteristically mystified. She was tapping her feet vigorously, and she hesitated before speaking. "Um. I'm not really sure about me. I mean, I love playing guitar and all. I really do. But I just can't say if I am going to be a professional. I know I want to go to college, but after that I'm not sure."

For the first time ever, I saw Lashley have a lapse in confidence. She was searching for words, chewing on the inside of her cheek. She noticed her wiggling feet and dropped them firmly to the floor, placing her hands on her knees.

"Fine, fine," Jason said softly. "That's why you're here–to explore music. You don't have to decide your future right now."

"It's just that . . ." Lashley was almost stuttering. She glanced at me and then looked back at Jason. "It's just that I am not sure what I want to be." She looked down at her knees, which were now knocking together. I couldn't figure out why she was so nervous and why she kept shooting me quick looks.

"Good. Enough said." Jason stacked all the papers together in a neat pile, and slapped his thighs, sighing. "Now let's talk about how you have been learning guitar. Lashley, what have you been doing with your teacher?"

Lashley sat up straighter and settled her legs. "Oh. My teacher, Perrin Isaac, is totally cool. When I first started, he taught me power chords. Soon we started jamming to Stevie

Ray Vaughn and Eric Clapton. He also taught me to read music. Now, every lesson we read music first, and then we jam."

"Great," said Jason. "So we can build on all that and work on your fingerstyle." He turned to me. "And Eric, what about you?"

I hesitated, embarrassed that I'd never had a teacher. My family couldn't afford it. What I wanted most in the world was a great guitarist to notice me and say, "Hey, kid. You're not bad. Lemme show you something. . . ."

I looked at Jason. Would he be the one? Would he know what I needed?

"Well, my uncle taught me some stuff," I said. "And I learned to read music in school. After that, I just hung out with other kids who took lessons, and I learned from them. Now I listen to recordings and try to play like old blues and jazz players."

"All right," said Jason. "That's cool. Self-taught like Django Reinhardt, the Gypsy guitarist. Hang out with other players, Eric, and try their techniques. But don't copy. You've got to find your own sound."

I relaxed. I had thought Jason would think I was lame for not having a real teacher. But he understood. I had this feeling I'd come to the right place.

"Yeah, okay," I said, suddenly feeling connected to him. "And who was your teacher?"

"Ah, my teacher?" Jason looked off into space. "My teacher is awesome. He's the kind of teacher who watches you play, listens with his eyes closed, and then says one small thing that blasts open your understanding about a piece of music. Suddenly you go from 'plink-plink-plink' to 'KABOOM,' and you can't figure out how that happened."

He looked at both of us and held his breath for a fraction of a second. I tried to imagine his teacher—"plink-plink-plink" to "KABOOM"; what an image. Who was this teacher?

Jason suddenly leaned sideways and grabbed the handle of his guitar case, which was leaning against the wall. He slid the case to the floor in front of him and opened the latches quickly, without looking, as if he'd done it a thousand times. Inside the case was a gorgeous resonator guitar with palm trees etched on the metal body. I had only seen pictures of those guitars.

Jason lifted the guitar out of the case and ran his left hand up the neck. "This belongs to my teacher, but he lets me use it whenever I want. Isn't it amazing?"

"Awesome! That's a National Style O resonator, isn't it?" I asked Jason.

"Right on the mark." Jason beamed. "Can you guess the year?"

Lashley made a face at me in disbelief. I shrugged my shoulders at her. "What? So I know guitars. You read novels; I read guitar books."

She frowned at me. I looked back at the guitar.

"Oh, man. What a cool guitar. Can I hold it?"

Jason handed me the guitar. I traced my fingers over the ebony fingerboard and imagined myself playing it in concert. "I'd say this is a 1935 or '36 because they stopped using the palm tree pattern after that. I bet it was really expensive back then."

"Whoa, Eric! You *are* a guitar freak," Jason said, smiling. "Back then it cost about sixty-five bucks, but my dad won it in a card game."

"A card game?" said Lashley. "Who would put up that guitar in a card game?"

"Well, that's the story," Jason said, crossing his arms in front of his chest.

I looked up at Jason and smiled. "So that means your father is your teacher, right?"

Jason's face opened with his soft grin. "You don't miss a beat, do you, Eric?"

I tossed my head, a little embarrassed but pleased that Jason had noticed.

"Yes, Old Samuel is my teacher. He learned to play like you, Eric, from hanging around other players. He loves this resonator guitar, which for a long time was his only friend. As soon as I was old enough to sit up and hold something without falling over, my father put a guitar in my hands."

"That's cool–jammin' with your own dad," I said, thinking about my father. "My dad is a contractor. He spends his life building things, and never listening to anything on the radio but sports. Doesn't matter what kind, just sports."

"Nothing wrong with that, Eric. You got to be who you are."

"I guess."

"At least your dad lets you come to music camp," Jason said. "Some kids don't have that chance."

"Yeah," I said, knowing he was right but still wishing my dad liked music.

Jason put his hand on my shoulder. "Eric, I think you and my father have to meet each other. He has a passion for guitars that saves his soul . . . just like your passion is saving yours."

I looked into Jason's eyes and knew what he meant. Guitar saves me. It's the one part of my life where everything feels okay. I'm not that hot in school, and I have trouble reading, but when I'm on guitar I never think about that other stuff. In my family, I'm the only one who's musical. That makes me a bit of a freak. My dad and brother are great athletes. My mom is into gardening and books. If I didn't have my guitar, my music, I might as well be cast off naked on an empty raft in the middle of the Pacific Ocean.

"Cool," I said to Jason. "When can I meet him?"

"Very soon," Jason said to me. "I'll make sure of it. Now, you two, there are a few camp details I have to tell you."

"Okay," said Lashley, looking wiggly again as if she was dying to get out of there.

"As for general camp rules, they're listed in your handbook. Read it tonight." Jason gave us each a handbook. "I trust you both to be sensible and not wander off where we cannot find you. During free periods, campers can go down to the wharf area in pairs as long as you sign out in the office. We'll be offering optional field trips so you can see something of San Francisco. For those, you also have to sign up in the office."

"What about Alcatraz?" I asked, leaning forward in excitement.

Amused, Jason jerked his head back a little and chuckled.

Lashley threw me a look that said, "Not Alcatraz again!"

"Yes, Alcatraz is the favorite field trip," Jason said. "So sign up right away. We'll also go to Chinatown, where my dad and I live."

"You live in Chinatown? Neat," said Lashley. "I'd rather go to Chinatown than Alcatraz."

Jason's eyes widened, and he tilted his head sideways to look closely at Lashley. "Really? Most kids love Alcatraz."

"Criminals aren't my thing," Lashley said with scorn.

Jason cleared his throat. "Okay," he said, shrugging. "Now, get on out of here and relax before the camp meeting and dinner. Check your schedules for tomorrow's individual lesson."

"Okay," Lashley said. We stood up to go.

"See you tonight," I said, walking out the door.

CHAPTER FOUR

Juan

"So, what was going on with you, Lash?" I asked as we walked down the hall of the music building. "You couldn't wait to get out of there."

"I don't know. I'm tired," Lashley said, being vague again. "As I said before, the car ride was exhausting." She was looking at the ground.

"I thought nothing wore you out."

"Wrong," she said harshly, walking determinedly toward the exit.

I felt a little jolt inside. I'd never heard Lashley sound mean before.

"Hey, what's bugging you? Did I say something wrong?"

Lashley stopped but wouldn't look up at me. "No, you didn't say . . . I mean, er, well, it's just that . . ."

"It's just what, Lashley?"

She hid her face from me. "It's just that you were so cool and smart in there, and I sounded like a dope."

"No, you didn't. What gave you that idea?"

"You sounded like a great guitarist–and you know everything about guitars. I sounded second rate and wishy-washy."

I didn't get why Lashley was so frustrated.

"Hey, you know as well as I do that we're equal on guitar. I love playing with you."

That didn't cheer her up.

"Lash, for me, music is everything. I don't have any other great talents like you do. If I didn't have music, I'd have nothing."

Lashley scowled. "Don't be so dramatic, Eric." She turned away and stomped down the hallway.

I scurried to keep up with her. "Hey. I'm not being dramatic. It's the truth."

"Yeah, sure," she said sarcastically. "Like you're some poor, neglected musical genius!"

I stopped suddenly and Lashley stopped again too, several steps ahead of me in front of the exit. She turned to look at me behind her. Her brow was tight, and her eyes red and narrowed.

I stared at her, amazed that we were arguing. "I never said I was a musical genius."

"You almost did," Lashley said.

"Lashley, you're good at everything. Me? I'm one dimensional. But, at least I have that one dimension. I'm holding on to it as tightly as I can."

Lashley turned away and started to push the door open. "Good. You do that."

She thrust herself out the exit.

I caught the door and held it open to watch Lashley march away. Her long hair swayed from side to side against her back.

"Whoa, Lash! What's going on?" I yelled.

She didn't stop.

I was stunned. I couldn't believe what she had just said. Lashley had never been like that before. What had happened in the music room? Why was she so upset? My mind swept over our conversation with Jason. I had no idea what was wrong, and suddenly I felt panicky without the anchor of her friendship. I felt very far from home.

I stood alone at the exit for who knows how long. My feet felt glued to the floor and my legs numb and stiff. Where should I go? I kept asking myself. What should I do next? Should I leave camp? Should I run back to Jason's office and talk to him about Lashley? Should I call home and talk to my parents?

I was stuck.

"Hey, kid," someone yelled from inside the building.

I looked down the hallway.

"What kind of guitar you got there?" the voice asked.

A short, dark-haired boy with bright brown eyes was walking toward me. He bounced slightly as he walked, and his short arms swung in quick arcs. His movements were so fast and jerky he looked as if he could have made sparks in the air.

"Who? Me?" I asked.

"You're the only other person around, right?" He came right up close to me.

"Who are you?"

He jutted out his chin and tightened his eyes. "Hey. I asked you first. What kind of guitar is that?" He leaned forward as if to take the guitar case from me.

I swung the case away from his grasp, and he jumped back in surprise.

"Protective, aren't we?" he said, peering into my face. I stepped back a little.

"It's a Fender Strat," I said, pulling the case up to my chest. "Why? What do you play?"

He laughed in a friendly way. "Ha. What do I play? The same . . . when I get the chance. But that's not often."

"Why not?"

"I'm broke," he said.

"So how do you play Fenders?"

"For Fenders, I go to a place in Haight-Ashbury where they let you try out new electrics. For acoustics–Froggy Bottoms are my favorite–I ferry across the bay to Schoenberg Guitars. Man, their selection is first rate."

"Okay" was all I said before he interrupted me. He was talking so fast I had to hold my breath to keep up with his words. His body jerked and bounced as he talked.

"I'm saving up every last drop of lawn-mowing and car-washing money. One day I'm gonna waltz myself into Schoenberg's and lay big bills on the counter. Won't those guys be surprised when their little Juanito hands them the gold?"

I was imagining this kid as a midget putting big bills onto the guitar shop counter as three tall sales clerks look down at him and laugh.

"Yeah. Their eyes on them are gonna just pop out. 'Hey, Juanito!' they're gonna say. 'Whadja do? Win the lottery?' And I'm gonna smile a big one and run my hands down the smooth face of my new guitar! I'll have trouble choosing 'tween a Fender or a Froggy Bottom, but I'll get over it. Or maybe I'll get both."

With his eyes closed, the boy was swaying side to side with the thought of having a new guitar. I was dumbfounded. I'd never laid eyes on this kid before, and he was talking to me as if I were his oldest friend. Strange kid . . . but I was drawn to him for some reason.

"Hey, I'm Juan Candello. Born on a small tropical island in the Atlantic Ocean but bred in hilly San Francisco. One of five Candello kids–four boys and a beautiful little sister. I was brought into this world to skip chemistry and history classes, and to spend all day playing lovely tunes for my fellow citizens of this planet!"

Juan sang all this out without taking a breath. "Now, who are you and where did your mighty fine girlfriend run off to?"

"She's not my girlfriend."

"Is that right?" he said, raising an eyebrow. "Well, good, because then maybe she can be mine."

"Yeah, well, I'm not too sure–"

"That's okay. You don't have to be sure. You can go along

and be dumb around beautiful girls, but that's not my style. So what's her name anyway, and where does she come from?"

"Hey, hold on. Slow down. I don't even know you." This kid was nuts, I thought.

"Man! You kiddin'? If I slow down, I'll never get anywhere in this world. Look at you. You're just standing here with this dumb look on your face, and you let your girlfriend run off on you like that. You're gonna rot here glued to the floor. Why don't you come along with me, and we'll jam together for a while? I bet we got some tunes we both know. What d'ya say?"

"You don't even know my name."

"So, what is it? And tell me your girlfriend's too in case you two split up for real. But don't be worrying about me. I'd never steal a girlfriend from a buddy. That's not my style."

"I'm Eric Wieman, from Massachusetts, and my friend is Lashley Moran from New Orleans," I said.

"New Orleans! You've got to be kiddin' me. That beautiful girl is from New Orleans? Home to all that jazz and blues and–Ah, man, New Orleans is where I'm going just as soon as I get my new Strat! You ever been there?"

"Yup. Just last winter, for the contest. That's how I got here. Lashley and I each won a Strat and the scholarship to camp."

Juan's thick black eyebrows lifted into an upside-down half-moon, and his jaw hung open for a second.

"Then you must be the dude people are talking about. The superstar whose whammy bar was busted off by that punk

Jordan Brooks. Last summer, he did that kind of thing here at camp too. He's a creep. Man, I heard all about you and Lashley. You two are already famous here. And I have to thank you for showing up Jordan Brooks. There are many of us who will kiss your feet. We don't miss that punk."

"Yeah, he was something," I said. "From the first moment I saw him I knew he was going to be trouble. I was always looking over my shoulder for him. He tried more than once to sabotage my performance. Good thing I don't have to deal with him anymore."

"Yeah, well, let's go find an empty practice room and play for a while. Then I'll let you in on the one kid here who won't be kissing your feet. Jordan had ONE friend at camp–Peter Mooring–and they were inseparable. Together they bullied half the kids here, and the teachers never witnessed it. Nobody was brave enough to squeal, so the deadly duo kept it up all summer. One little kid actually quit camp because he was so scared of those two. Once Peter finds out who YOU are, he will give you big-time trouble."

"Oh, great," I said, groaning at the thought of another bully. "That's all I need . . . another nemesis."

"Another what?" Juan asked me as we walked outside to find a place to play guitar.

"Enemy. Another enemy seeking vengeance," I said, shaking my head.

CHAPTER FIVE

Old Samuel

At six o'clock that evening, after jamming together on some old Clapton tunes, Juan and I walked into the hostel living room for our first general meeting. Lashley was already sitting on the floor with many of the other campers, and she waved me over to the empty space near her. I looked at Juan to see if he wanted to sit together near Lashley, and from the excited look on his face I could tell he couldn't wait to be introduced. I didn't want to sit next to Lashley. My head was still ringing with her mean words. My stomach muscles were fluttering.

"I've got to meet this New Orleans girl," Juan whispered to me.

"Well, she may not be in the best of moods," I said.

"Ah! That's nothing," Juan whispered back. "I'm a pro at cheering people up."

We sat down next to her–Juan between Lashley and me.

Lashley smiled her normal smile when I introduced her to Juan, but she was definitely avoiding eye contact with me. I was still miffed at her and wanted an explanation, but she seemed charmed by Juan. Talking to him, she acted all giggly, which isn't normal for her. I decided to go along with her game until I could talk to her alone. I stayed quiet and just listened to them babble until the camp director, a tall, lanky woman with chestnut hair and a scarf around her neck, stood up to make an announcement.

"Hello, everyone," she said, opening her arms wide. "I am Marty Rosenberg, the director of the Quickfinger Guitar Camp. I welcome all of you, and I know we're going to have an amazing camp session. I see many familiar faces and am glad to have those people back for another summer. And to those of you who are new, we are happy to have you here. I know you bring with you great musical talent.

"Tonight I will introduce you to our camp faculty, and then we'll have a short performance before dinner. I know you are all hungry, so this meeting will be brief."

As Ms. Rosenberg was introducing each guitar instructor, I looked around the room at the other kids. Although I had seen most of them at our picnic lunch, I hadn't spoken to any of them except Juan. I wondered who played classical guitar, electric, or acoustic bluegrass. Which kids were as determined as I was to become a professional, and where was Peter Mooring? I planned to steer clear of him.

As I stared at all the faces in the room, my gaze rested on an old man sitting in an armchair on the far right side of the room, out of the way. He was paying attention to what was going on, but he looked too old to be an instructor. His pale blue eyes flickered with what looked like amusement.

The old man had a full head of soft, white hair combed in a wave over the right side of his forehead, and he wore a blue work shirt over blue jeans that hung loosely over his skinny legs. His legs were crossed, and his foot tapped rhythmically in the air as if he was listening to some song in his head. Every couple of minutes he coughed a hollow, raspy cough that sounded deep and chronic. For some unknown reason, I couldn't take my eyes off him.

The old man turned toward me, caught my stare, and smiled at me. I smiled back quickly, but then turned away, embarrassed to have been caught staring. When I peeked again at the old man, he caught me a second time and was still grinning. I laughed aloud that time, and the people around me, including Lashley and Juan, turned to look at me.

"What's so funny?" Lashley leaned in front of Juan toward me and whispered.

"Nothing," I answered, pretending to concentrate on the teachers in front of us. I could feel Lashley staring at me, waiting for more of an answer, but I wasn't going to give one. I heard her make a long sigh, and then she shrugged at Juan and looked up front. Ms. Rosenberg was just introducing Jason Parker.

"This year we are proud to have as our new instructor the talented Jason Parker, whom many of you know from his concerts around town. You may also have seen him perform in his father's band. And with us tonight is Jason's father, Samuel

Parker–affectionately known as Old Samuel–sitting over there by the fireplace. Samuel, could you wave at us from over there?"

All heads in the room turned toward the old man with white hair, who was still grinning. He waved a crooked arm at the campers.

"Cool," Lashley whispered. "Jason's dad."

"Mmmm," I mumbled, staring again at the old man. So, that's Jason's father, I said to myself. I never would have guessed. Jason's eyes and skin were so brown and Asian, but his father was fair and somewhat freckled. I could see a similarity in their square jaws and in the way they smiled. There was something about Old Samuel that mesmerized me. Sitting over there, smiling away at the kids, he looked so off on a distant cloud and so content. I couldn't wait to meet him to see if Jason was right–to see if Old Samuel and I had something in common.

Ms. Rosenberg was waving at Jason's dad and giggling. She looked giddy over the old guy. She tilted her head and took in a deep breath of air, and I thought she was going to faint.

"Jason and his father have so, so kindly agreed to play a couple of tunes as a way of opening up our camp session this summer. For those of you who have never heard these two play, you're in for a real treat."

Some kids murmured, and somebody shouted, "Yeah!"

Ms. Rosenberg looked at Jason. "Are you two ready, Jason?"

Jason leaped from his seat and walked over to his dad. Then he turned toward the kids and said, "Why don't you all turn this way, and dad and I will play from this side of the room. It will be easier."

We all shifted ourselves to the right while Jason pulled out the gorgeous resonator guitar and handed it to his father. He opened another case, pulled out a banjo, and sat down on the empty stool next to his dad. As Jason tuned his instrument, Old Samuel started to run his knobby fingers up and down the neck of his. Then he broke into a slow blues riff. He looked stiff and ancient, but his fingers moved with grace. He closed his eyes and played alone for a few minutes before starting into a modern, funky, bluegrass rhythm. His guitar whined, and then Jason's banjo jumped in and raced in short, punctuated phrases. One instrument leaped over the other, the music sliding on and then kicking the air. The sound washed over us in layers of melody, and we were silent, swaying, and enraptured.

I'd never heard this kind of playing live and up close. Jason played effortlessly, but Old Samuel had just the right touch at every moment. The beat jumped through his body and his fingers and moved directly into the guitar. As old and crooked as he looked, he was one with his instrument. The sound was fresh and exciting, but relaxed, easy. I felt as if my whole life had occurred so that I could be there at that moment to hear that music. KABOOM! As if I had been whacked on the head, suddenly I knew that Jason wasn't the teacher I wanted . . . Samuel was.

Jason and Samuel played five songs and then called it quits. Old Samuel looked so bouncy after the fifth song that he probably could have gone on for another five hours. But Jason stopped him and took away the guitar. Samuel grinned at the campers and pretended to play more on an air guitar. Some of us laughed, and Samuel made a monkey face, with bouncing, laughing eyes.

One boy shouted, "One more song!" And the campers broke into loud applause.

"That's my dad, folks!" Jason shouted as he waved at the kids to stop clapping. "He could go on forever. He even plays in his sleep. I see those fingers moving all day and all night. Doesn't matter how tired the guy is. But now, we've got to break for dinner."

Samuel chuckled with his dry lips slightly parted, and he waved at the campers again. The effort caused him to start coughing, and Ms. Rosenberg, looking concerned, brought him a glass of water.

"Let's hear it again for Jason and Old Samuel, everybody," said Ms. Rosenberg. "Two of the very best!"

I clapped hard and cheered for my new inspiration. I had to meet Samuel right away and talk to him. I needed to get closer to his music.

CHAPTER SIX

Peter

After listening to Samuel and Jason, I walked to dinner with an upbeat rhythm. Inside, I was rocking just as Samuel had rocked in his chair in the camp living room. I really knew what people meant by having music constantly on the brain, constant rhythm coming up through the soles of the feet. Samuel has that, and so do I. We could talk the same language. I just had to get to know him.

As hungry as I was for dinner–and I'm always hungry–I would rather have stayed and played guitar with Jason and Samuel than get up and move along to the cafeteria line with Lashley and Juan. I didn't feel like asking Lashley again what was bothering her, and I didn't feel like being friendly to her until she apologized. We avoided each other, but Juan was there in the middle, talking to both of us. I know he was trying to pull us back together.

"Hey, you two," Juan said. "Wait 'til you see the spread they put on in the cafeteria. You always think of camp food as rotten, don't you?" Juan nodded his head for us as he spoke. "Well, here's where the Quickfinger Guitar Camp outdoes itself.

They've got the best Californian, east-west, fusion-groovin', savory edibles I've ever eaten. If only my parents could cook like that, I might turn into another muscle-bound, handsome-hunk Ricky Martin. I'd flex my arm and leg muscles every time I hit the stage in front of ten million screamin' girls. Whoa!"

Lashley laughed. Some kids behind us cracked up too.

"You wish!" Lashley said, smiling at Juan.

"Well," said Juan, lifting up his arms and flexing his sinewy muscles. "I can dream, can't I?"

Lashley squeezed Juan's arm muscle and then flexed her own. There was no contest. Lashley was definitely stronger.

"Dream on, Juan," I said, picking up a cafeteria tray. "All our muscles are in our guitar fingers."

Lashley walked next to Juan and bumped into him, laughing at his jokes. I watched them from behind, and looked around to see if Jason and Samuel were coming to dinner. I couldn't spot them.

As we three walked down the food line, each with a tray, Juan grabbed at dishes of food and put them on our trays.

"You've got to try this," Juan kept saying as he filled up our trays.

"Juan!" said Lashley as she returned a few dishes to the display counter. "I can't possibly eat stew and spaghetti and carrot cake and apple pie."

A bunch of kids in line stared at our trays and scrunched up their faces.

"Ah, come on," said Juan. "Sure you can, Lashley. And what you don't finish, I will. We're growing kids, you know. We need all the nourishment we can get to express our true musical talents. You certainly don't want to weaken right in the middle of a mind-bending solo, do you?"

Juan put a bowl of fruit on Lashley's tray, and she left it there.

"Hey, Juan!" yelled a tall boy behind me. "Keep it moving, bud. We're all hungry here. And this year, leave some food for the rest of us, will ya?"

The boy tossed his head to the side and rolled his eyes. Juan obviously had a reputation for eating a lot, but nobody seemed to dislike him. I suspected Juan had a way with jokes that kept him on everyone's good side. Except maybe for Peter Mooring. From what Juan had told me, nobody was on Peter's good side. I still didn't know which one Peter was, but I kept my eyes open for him. Juan had said Peter was short, thick shouldered, red haired, and unsmiling.

Seated in the hostel dining room at one of its long, rectangular tables, I paid little attention to my spaghetti and salad. Instead, I scanned the room to get the feel of the place, and I stared out the window at the cypress trees behind the building. For a moment I felt very alone, lost in a place with unfamiliar sounds and colors. But then I looked back inside the dining room again, and my mind shifted.

Music camp. This is what I had always wanted–teachers who would understand why I loved music. I was right in the middle of it all, and this was my chance to become really good on guitar. I looked for Jason and Old Samuel. They were sitting a few tables away, surrounded by a gang of kids all leaning over their trays and talking. I wanted to be over there. I wanted Old Samuel to notice me. I wanted to talk to him about guitars and riffs and old blues players. But, as much as I wanted all that, I didn't dare go over there to sit with them. I didn't know any of the kids.

With that thought, I turned back to Juan and Lashley, who were seated across from me, and listened to their conversation about the other campers. Juan was giving Lashley the lowdown on the little groups of friends. He also warned her about Peter Mooring.

"Hey, foggy brain Eric is going to join us again," Juan said to Lashley as he elbowed her softly in the arm. "Where've you been, Mr. Silver Strat? Dreamin' up love songs?" Juan chuckled and made faces at me to get me to laugh.

"Nah," I said to Juan. "I was just noticing how different the trees are in California. They're nothing like the trees in Vermont."

"Trees? You've been thinking about trees?" Juan said, his face all screwed up. "Who are you? Paul Bunyan or something?"

I shrugged. "My grandfather loves trees."

"Oh, yeah?" said Juan, nodding. "Mine likes engines."

"Grandpa John would love pictures of California trees. I should get one of those cheap throwaway cameras."

"That's cool." Juan nodded his head vigorously. "Grandpops are cool. I can show you some amazing San Francisco trees, if you want. Tall eucalyptus trees that smell so good."

"Great," I said. "When?"

Juan thought for a second and said, "We have downtime from four to six almost every afternoon. Kids read, write letters, or hang out. Maybe next week, after we're settled, I'll take you on an afternoon walking tour."

"Sure," I said, thinking about Grandpa John.

"Me too," said Lashley. "I love adventures."

I looked away from Lashley, stuck my elbows on the table, and dropped my head into my right palm. Lashley was really bugging me at that moment, but I didn't know what to do about it. She was getting all buddy-buddy with Juan, almost as if she were silently telling me she didn't need me. But then she went and invited herself along on my tree adventure as if nothing strange had happened between us.

I wondered–should I just forget about how she had acted in the hallway and be nice to her, or should I ignore her? Should I let her know I was ticked off or not? I couldn't make up my mind what to do, but then I thought of something.

"Hey, Juan," I said. "What do you know about Alcatraz? Is it as cool as it looks in the movies?"

Lashley sighed and rolled her eyes. "Not Alcatraz again, Eric," she said under her breath. I ignored her.

"Hey, Alcatraz is cool," I said loudly. "Right, Juan?"

Juan took my bait without knowing it. "Ah, man, Alcatraz is amazing. I go every year. I love it." Juan turned to Lashley. "You gotta go to Alcatraz, Lashley."

Lashley shook her head and glared at me. I knew she was annoyed. I was satisfied that she knew I was bringing up Alcatraz just because she didn't want to go.

"To go to Alcatraz is to glorify spineless criminals," Lashley said. "Gee. Let's all congratulate Al Capone and Machine Gun Kelly. Isn't it cool that they extorted money and murdered people?" Lashley's nostrils flared. She jabbed her fork fiercely into a sliced tomato.

We were all quiet for a moment.

I started feeling a little guilty for rubbing Lashley's nose into Alcatraz.

But then I didn't care. I looked over at Jason and Samuel's table again and wished I were with them.

Juan ate hungrily, all hunched down over his food. Lashley sat chewing the inside of her cheek.

Suddenly I noticed a red-haired boy standing behind Juan's chair. He had come out of nowhere.

"So, Juanito, big mouth!" said the boy, breathing down Juan's neck. "I see you found some new friends pretty quick." Looking at me, the boy went on. "Lousy choice of company," he snarled.

I didn't know if he was talking about me or Juan.

Juan looked at me and mouthed the words *Peter Mooring.*

He didn't have to tell me. From Juan's earlier description, I had figured out who the boy was. Lashley looked at Juan and then at me and nodded slowly.

"Hello, Peter," said Juan in an exaggerated, sarcastic tone of voice. He didn't look up or turn around to see the red-haired boy. "I didn't think you'd show up this summer without your bodyguard. Weren't you guys glued together last year? How'd they separate you? Too bad for you that Jordan was finally stopped. We all knew he'd be caught one day. And so will you, if you keep it up, Peter."

Peter's eyes shrank inside his sockets, and his jaw tightened behind his thin, down-turned lips. His face was closed and hard.

"Oh, Juan. No need to be so harsh in front of pretty girls like this one," Peter hissed, touching Lashley's ponytail and flicking it off her shoulders.

Lashley swung around and stood up to look Peter in the eye. "Hey. Who do you think you are? Touch my hair again, and you'll regret it."

"Will you listen to that?" Peter announced loudly, looking at the kids around us, who had stopped eating and were now staring at Lashley and Peter. One kid rolled his eyes and groaned the words "Peter Mooring."

Peter stepped back a little to look Lashley up and down. "Oh, my," he said. "Juan has got a tough new girlfriend." Peter looked Lashley in the eye. "I wouldn't try me, little girl. You might end up in the camp infirmary begging the nurse to let you go home."

Lashley took one step closer to Peter and looked him straight in the face. "I wouldn't count on it," she said very slowly. "I'm not afraid of you."

And she turned her back on Peter, picked up her tray, and walked away without looking back.

"Sassy!" said Peter, raising his eyebrows and crossing his arms in front of his chest. "I can see what you like in her, Juanito!"

I glared at Peter from across the table. "She's a champion," I said, immediately regretting I had opened my mouth.

"In what? Fingernail polishing?" Peter asked, looking over at me. "And what's it to you? Are you her little brother?"

Juan stood up, cleared his throat, and lifted his tray from the table. He nodded at me to do the same. With a sideways jerk of the head, he indicated that we should get out of there.

"Yeah, that's right," I lied to Peter. "I'm her little brother."

I stood up slowly, extending my body way above Peter's head, and watched his eyes follow my face upward. Being tall sometimes has its advantages. I picked up my tray, turned away from Peter, and walked with Juan to the conveyor belt for the dirty trays. I didn't look back.

"We're in luck," Juan whispered to me. "Peter still doesn't know who you are."

I nodded and leaned toward Juan's ear. "Yeah, let's keep it that way."

CHAPTER SEVEN

Moody Intro

That night, after dinner, all the camp kids went to their dorms early to unpack their sleeping bags and settle into their bunks. Lashley's dorm was down the hall from mine, and I didn't see her again after dinner. That was just as well. I was ready to crash into bed because my body was on Eastern time though the clock was on Pacific time. I climbed up to my top bunk and pulled an old T-shirt and sweatpants from my backpack. I could hardly keep my eyes open while I changed clothes.

"You been here before?" I heard someone ask me softly.

I looked at the top bunk closest to mine and realized the boy on it was talking to me. He was sitting cross-legged and leaning over some stationery, writing.

"Who, me?" I asked him.

"Yeah," he said, shyly. His brown bangs hung over his eyes.

"No. I've never been here before."

"Me either," he said, nodding his head. He sounded sad.

"Seems okay, though," I said to encourage him.

"I guess," he answered, writing something more.

"Who are you writing?" I asked.

"My sister," he said. "She's back in Wyoming, where I'm from."

"Wyoming? Cool," I said. "I've only seen pictures of Wyoming. Is it as wide open as it looks?"

The boy smiled and swung his bangs out of his face. "Yup. I guess it is, especially if you live on a ranch like I do. Feels real strange to be in a city. I've never been in a big city before."

I wanted to talk to this kid, but I was falling asleep sitting up. "Yeah. It must be strange." My voice was trailing off. "Hey. You know, I'm from Massachusetts, where it's three hours later than here. I've got to drop my head on my pillow right now or I won't survive, if you know what I mean. What's your name?"

"Spencer Boyd," he said, chewing on his pen.

"Well, I'm Eric Wieman. I'd like to hear all about Wyoming. Would you tell me later?"

Spencer nodded again and gave me a small wave. He went back to writing, and I slipped into my sleeping bag. I must have fallen asleep in two minutes because I don't remember another thing about that first night.

The next day, I got up and went to breakfast long before the other kids. Spencer was asleep when I climbed down from my bunk, so I didn't bother him. The cafeteria was almost empty, and I chose a seat next to the picture window again so I could look out at the trees as I ate my granola and muffin. My head felt empty, and I breathed in all the unrecognizable smells of Fort Mason.

The other kids started trickling in after I had finished eating. First Juan came to my table, and then Lashley. Nobody was talkative that morning, not even Juan. Lashley's face was cloudy, as if she might have been crying during the night. I avoided eye contact with her again, but doing so made me feel like a rowboat untied from its dock. I didn't really want to keep our fight going, but I didn't know how to break the tension.

"Everybody sleep okay?" I asked.

Lashley and Juan both shrugged and muttered, "Yeah."

"So I guess we'll be in class all day today, right?" I asked Juan, who was the expert on camp.

He grunted, and I took that for a yes. I decided to stand up and clear my tray.

"Well, I'm going to put new strings on my guitar now and figure out where I'm supposed to be today. I'll see you guys at lunch. Okay?"

Again, no words from them, just grunts. Lashley lifted her eyes for a second as if to say good-bye, but looked down again quickly at her breakfast. I had thought we'd be going to classes together, but I had been wrong.

That first full day of camp, I had to find my way around Fort Mason alone. The music classes were spread out in different buildings, and I used a map to figure out where I needed to be. I trekked from one class to the next–music theory, fingerstyle class with Jason, percussion class, and composition–moving in a kind of fog. I talked to a few other kids in my classes, but I didn't see Lashley or Juan all day. We must have had lunch scheduled at different times, and I felt lonely.

By late afternoon, I was tired again, and I went back to my bunk to relax. Spencer was there, writing another letter, and we chatted about his growing up in Wyoming.

"You really ride in rodeos?" I asked him in amazement.

"Sure," he said. "All my buddies do too. In Wyoming, most of us ranch kids learn to lasso wooden horses when we're toddlers, and calves when we're about seven or eight. Herding cattle and competing in rodeos–that's just what we do. That, and star gazing. You just can't believe the open skies of Wyoming. I've never seen as many stars anywhere else."

"How old are you, Spencer?" I asked.

"Eleven," he answered softly. "But don't tell them other guys. They might tease me for being the youngest here."

"Okay. I won't," I said. "I'm just amazed that you can rope steer and ride through barrels, and you're only eleven."

"It's not unusual in Wyoming," he said, shyly.

"So how did you learn to play guitar?" I imagined cowboys singing around a campfire.

"My daddy taught me. When your ranch is as far away from things as ours is, you don't get to town very often. Going to school is tough enough. And when school's over, I've got plenty of chores and homework and all. I never took lessons or nothing, except from my daddy."

"I never took lessons either," I said. "So we have something in common. But my dad doesn't care about music."

"Too bad," Spencer said, going back to writing.

At six o'clock, Spencer and I went down the hall for dinner. We joined the cafeteria line, and when we entered the dining room, we realized the tables were set up for our special camp groups. Each table was marked by a small flag with an instructor's name on it. Each camper was to sit with his or her main instructor. Spencer and I had to part, he to Don's table, where Juan was already seated, and I to Jason's, at the table by my favorite window.

"I guess we won't be seeing much of each other if we're in separate groups, " I told Spencer.

His face fell, and I wondered if he should have come to camp so young.

"See ya," he said quietly.

"Yeah," I said. "We can always talk at night in our bunks."

Spencer nodded and slumped away silently.

I looked at Jason's table and was thrilled to see Old Samuel there too. Lashley and some other kids were already there eating, and I walked over to join them. Sitting down next to Lashley, I smiled at Jason across the table and then stuck out my hand to Samuel. I had to grab the chance to meet him.

"I'm Eric Wieman," I said to Old Samuel. "Your playing last night was fantastic. I'm really glad to meet you."

Old Samuel smiled and gripped my hand strongly. "Nice to meet you, Eric," he said.

"Do you teach here too?" I asked him. "I'd like to learn some of the things you played last night."

Samuel laughed in a raspy voice. "No, I'm not an official instructor here. Jason just brings me along on a leash. Keeps me out of trouble." He laughed even harder.

Jason cocked his head at Samuel and raised his eyebrows. To me he said, "Dad doesn't like my cooking, so I bring him here for a good dinner."

"Oh," I said to Samuel, disappointed that he wouldn't be teaching us. "I was hoping to learn your fingerstyle."

Samuel nodded at me. Jason looked at Samuel and then at me. "Don't worry, Eric. You'll learn a lot this summer. Samuel will be around. I'm sure you two can play together sometime."

I imagined sitting down with Samuel and getting the chance to try out his resonator guitar. "Great," I said. "It's so cool to have real teachers."

I began to eat my dinner and then I realized I hadn't said hello to Lashley. Suddenly I was tired of our tension and decided to be friendly.

"How was it today?" I asked Lashley as I dug into my mashed potatoes.

"Good," she said. I think I saw relief on her face.

"I didn't see you the whole day after breakfast."

"I know. That was weird."

"Do you think we'll be in any of the same classes?" I asked.

"I think we have jazz band together tomorrow."

"Good," I said. "I'd hate to come all this way and not spend any time in camp together." At that moment, I knew I meant what I said. I really wanted to stay friends with Lashley.

"Yeah, I know," Lashley said as she turned her head around to watch something happening behind us.

"What's going on?" I asked her.

"Peter and Juan are sparring again," she said.

"Poor Juan," I whispered, not turning around. "He's got Peter in his group, I guess."

"I don't think so," Lashley said. "Don't look now but guess who is on his way toward us."

"Oh, great," I said under my breath. "He's in our group?" I held my fork in the air, stuck between bites of food.

Lashley ducked her head and went back to eating. "Ignore him," she said firmly.

Jason noticed Peter and called him to our table. "Peter, glad you could make it."

Peter scowled and sat down heavily right next to Lashley on her other side. She didn't flinch, but kept on eating as if nothing had happened. I tried to do the same by acting very interested in the colors of my salad.

Jason cleared his throat and looked around the table. "Gang, I don't know if you have all met each other yet. I brought us together tonight so you could see who is in your main instruction group. Our last arrival is Peter Mooring, a fine electric guitar player from Los Angeles."

Jason beamed at Peter, whose head was hanging over his tray. Peter gave a flicker of a proud smile and then went back to scowling. Jason continued his introductions.

"Peter told me that he was here last year, so he knows the ropes. He has been runner-up twice in the Quickfinger Guitar Contest, but he missed it this year because he broke his arm. Bad luck, Peter!"

Peter shrugged as if a broken arm was nothing and then ignored everyone as he ate. Jason then introduced the other kids around the table: Daniel, Allison, Rebecca, Gunter, John, Nelson, and Tenzin. I don't remember all the details Jason told us except that Gunter and Tenzin were international students–Gunter from Germany, and Tenzin from Nepal. Gunter is really, really tall, left handed, and from Berlin; Tenzin is shorter than the rest of us, handsome with rich brown eyes and skin, and is the very first electric guitar player in his school in Nepal. His home is up in a village near Mount Everest, but he goes to school in Kathmandu. He came to America with an international music exchange program.

"And last up are these two, Lashley Moran and Eric Wieman," Jason announced, pointing at us.

Just then I realized that Jason was going to tell everyone who we were. I panicked and wanted to run from the dining room. Peter was just about to find out we were the ones who caught

Jordan Brooks trying to sabotage my performance at the QG Contest. I was sure we were in for big trouble.

"Forget it," Lashley whispered, knowing what I had been thinking. "He would have found out anyway."

Jason went on. "Lashley and Eric tied for first place in this year's competition. Let's congratulate them."

A few of the kids at the table applauded for Lashley and me, but I couldn't even look up. I was afraid to see Peter's expression and I was sure we were doomed to a whole summer of Peter Plague.

When I finally lifted my eyes, I saw Peter raise his eyebrows at Lashley. His shoulders looked as if they might have stiffened a bit, but he was quiet, and his face gave away nothing of his thoughts. I didn't trust him one bit. I figured he was the type to act sophisticated and polite around adults, but then go back to bullying whenever the counselors weren't around. I was itching to finish the meeting.

I glanced at Old Samuel, who was swaying and had his eyes closed. The wrinkles on his face drew his skin down into a sad but gentle expression. He must have felt my eyes on him because suddenly he opened his and looked right at me. His blue eyes were watery and cloudy, but they seemed to look deep inside me.

Old Samuel glanced at Peter and mumbled something to him. Then he looked back at me and reached across the table to pat my arm. It was a weird gesture, and Lashley stared at Samuel's hand. Then she looked up at me as if wanting an explanation. I wondered if Samuel were a mind reader. I looked at him. He seemed to know somehow that Peter bothered me. I'm not sure why I believed that. I just saw it all in his face.

"Son, why don't we break out of this place an' sit in the livin' room," Old Samuel said to me. "It's crowded in here, ain't it?"

Lashley looked at me with a confused face, her mouth twisted to one side. I looked at her blankly and then back at Old Samuel.

"Sure!" I said to Samuel. "That'd be cool." And before I could change my mind and stay in the dining room, I got up and cleared my tray and Samuel's. Samuel got up too and hobbled around the table to lead me out.

I stopped for a second and glanced back at Lashley. Her face looked kind of unsure, her eyes wide and quivering.

"Lash," I said. "Come find us when you're done. We'll be in the living room."

I waited for an answer, but she didn't say anything. She looked back down at her tray.

"Okay. See ya," I said finally. She didn't respond.

And then I turned and joined Samuel in the hallway outside the dining room. Together we walked down the hall, and Samuel began asking me about my family and home. I started by telling him about my Grandpa John.

CHAPTER EIGHT

Feeling Alcatraz

I couldn't persuade Lashley to come out to Alcatraz with me because, number one, she was mad at me for leaving her at dinner and hanging out with Samuel on the second night of camp. And, number two, she thought I was making "heroes out of horrid convicts," as she put it, which wasn't true. My dad and I talked a lot about old gangsters, but we really didn't think of them as heroes.

In the end, it was Juan who persuaded Lashley to go. She finally relented when he told her she'd be crazy not to see the place. She was only going along because she didn't want Juan to think she was uncool. I knew she didn't want to be with me on that ferry to the island.

On the twelve-minute boat ride out to Alcatraz Island, Lashley paced inside the cabin with her blue rain jacket zippered up tight. She also bought a hot chocolate but didn't drink it. I wanted to be on the top deck with Jason and our group, but Lashley had asked me to keep her company below, so there I was. Sitting by a window, I watched white caps on the water and rain splattering against the windows. A few seagulls flew alongside the boat, looking for food from the passengers.

"I know. I know it's just a museum," Lashley said as she walked the length of the café deck for the hundredth time. "But there is something dark and evil about a place where desperate criminals once lived. You know . . . all those tormented thoughts collected on one island. Imagine what those demented minds left behind in the air."

"Come on, Lashley," I said. "You're beginning to sound like some New Age ya-ya."

"Well," said Lashley, disgruntled and moody, "it's no weirder than your not liking people to touch your guitar in case they damage the aura, or whatever."

I grunted. She had a good point there. I never liked people to mess with my guitar. I am definitely superstitious about some things.

"Maybe people *DO* leave behind shadows of their thoughts," she said, swinging her head away from me and marching to the ladies' room.

I felt confused about Lashley again. I didn't understand why she was so unpredictable ever since that first meeting with Jason. One minute she was laughing and as playful as she had been in New Orleans, and the next minute she was worried or conflicted. Something had definitely changed about her, but I didn't want to ask again what was wrong. When she returned from the bathroom, I just kept quiet and gave her space.

When the ferry docked on Alcatraz Island, my pulse began to race, and I wanted to sprint up the hill to the cell house. Jason waited on the dock for all the camp kids and then called our group together. Jumping up on a cement bench, Jason waved everyone in close. Chilled and damp in the gray drizzle, we shivered and listened to Jason's instructions. He told us to stay in pairs and to be back at the dock in three hours.

After picking up our tour tape players, Lashley and I put on our headphones and followed our group toward the cell house. I wanted to keep our distance from Peter, so we walked very slowly and let him get ahead. As we hiked up the hill from the dock, we could see remnants of an Alcatraz past. Concrete walls were crumbling, and the former warden's house was a shell of itself, but you could easily imagine the place with barbed wire and locked gates all around it. I wished my dad could have been with me.

Our tapes started, and we followed the directions of the narrator telling us to move this way and that through the cell house, which was crowded with tourists. On the tape you could hear the recorded sounds of former prison life–clanking gates, rumbling voices, shrill whistles, and footsteps tapping down the once polished concrete floors. These sound effects were so real that I almost expected to run into a group of prisoners at any moment.

Lashley and I stayed together as we turned down the main corridor of cells, called "Broadway." This ran between B-Block and C-Block, where most of the ordinary Alcatraz prisoners had been jailed. As we stepped slowly down "Broadway," we gawked at the three tiers of cells. Each cell was exactly like the next, each with a cot and blanket and pillow, a seatless toilet behind the cot, and a small sink with cold running water. On the right wall were a fold-down table and a seat where prisoners could read, write letters, draw, or do whatever they needed a table for. And that was it. No radio. No cubby for personal belongings. No decoration.

"Hey," I said to Lashley, stopping my tape and pulling off my headphones. I tilted my head to indicate that Lashley should pull off her headphones too.

"Doesn't Jason have the word *Broadway* painted on his music room door? Do you think he means this Broadway?"

Lashley thought for a second. "That's odd. I thought the word on his door referred to New York's Broadway. We'll have to ask him."

We both looked up to see if Jason was near us. He wasn't, so we put our headphones on again and continued to walk down the corridor.

Touring the cell house, I let my mind become a mental movie of prison life in Alcatraz. I tried to imagine being locked in a cell with only my own mind for company, with heavy thoughts of my crime. How would I feel living at the mercy of men who didn't like me and being told when to eat, when to sleep, what to wear, when to bathe, when to breathe fresh air? Would I survive? Would I bang my head against the wall and scream to be let out? Would I plan escape? And then I had the worst thought of all–what if I couldn't play guitar, and didn't have music? I know I'd go nuts. I'd lose my hold on life. I'd have no reason to live.

Looking into an isolation cell where prisoners had been held in total darkness, I got a strange urge to walk inside. I felt a pull in my gut drawing me into the dark to see what it was like in there. I held my breath and stepped in slowly.

Suddenly Lashley grabbed my arm forcefully and pulled me out.

"Are you nuts?" she shouted, yanking my arm until it hurt. "Get out of there."

I almost toppled over from Lashley's pull.

"Okay. Okay," I said calmly. "I was just curious."

"Curious?" she said. "About what?"

"Okay, Lashley," I said, wondering myself why I had felt pulled to go in. "I just wanted to know what it felt like to be in there."

"I can't believe you sometimes," Lashley said, shaking her head and adjusting her headphones.

We walked quickly to catch up with the tape and stopped in front of cells where infamous prisoners had plotted escapes. In one cell, Lashley and I saw the dummy head used by one of the three men who had dug out of their cells. I was excited to see it, and I wanted to tell Dad.

I took off my headphones and elbowed Lashley, who pulled one side of her headphones off her ear.

"This is the story I was telling you that first day here on the pier. Remember?"

"No. What story?" Lashley said, looking blankly at me.

"The one they made the Clint Eastwood movie about. The movie Dad and I watched before I left. I told you about it."

Lashley shrugged and put the ear cuff back on. "Sorry. I don't remember," she said, turning away and continuing the tour.

She doesn't remember, I said to myself. How can she not remember? We had a whole conversation about the prisoners who might have made it to freedom. What was going on with Lashley? She was like a totally different human being from the one I knew in New Orleans. I watched her walk away without waiting for me. I put my headphones back on and jogged to catch up with her.

Walking around the old prisoner dining room, we ran into a park ranger who volunteered to take about twenty tourists up to the hospital floor of the prison. Lashley tilted her head at me, unsure about going upstairs, but I nudged her along.

"Come on," I said. "This is our chance to see stuff most people don't see."

She shrugged and followed me reluctantly.

The park ranger smiled at Lashley and then spoke. "Now, if anyone is uncomfortable about being locked into the upstairs unit, turn around now. Or, if anyone is in a hurry, please do not come along." The guard looked at our group and said, "If we're all game, follow me."

He turned to a little boy and handed him a giant key. He let the boy unlock the gate to the stairway and lock it again after we had all passed through. The ranger patted the boy on the head, and then grinned at me. He was old and friendly, but he had a hint of menace in his eyes when the gate was locked behind us. I chuckled at him, but Lashley was chewing on the inside of her cheek and squinting at me.

"It's okay, Lashley. He's just trying to be funny."

"Warped sense of humor," she said.

Upstairs, the ranger showed us the old pharmacy that still smelled of iodine, an operating room, an X-ray room, a bathing room for sick inmates, a large observation room for mentally ill prisoners, and one long, empty cell that had been occupied by Robert Stroud, the so-called Birdman of Alcatraz. Stroud had been loud, volatile, and disliked by most of the guards. Because he often disrupted prison routine, he was confined upstairs away from the other prisoners.

As Lashley and I followed the park ranger back downstairs to the door that opened into the dining area, I caught a smell in the hospital ward that was sharp and bleak. I wondered how strong that smell must have been when mixed with the thick odors of prisoner sweat and fear. Something about the smell brought up a feeling in me that was pleasant and unpleasant at the same time. I felt the warmth of having a close-knit family, but a strange fear that something or someone could take it all away from me at any time. The thought made my stomach muscles tighten.

Before Lashley and I headed back to the dock, we stopped in the Alcatraz bookstore. I was picking out postcards and souvenirs for my dad while Lashley, as always, hunted through all the books in the crowded store.

"Hey, look at this one," Lashley said, showing me a book. "It was written by a prisoner and lists all the different escape attempts. Your dad might like it."

I took the book from Lashley and flipped through the pages of photographs. "The back cover says the author finished high school in prison and then got a job as an X-ray technician."

Lashley shrugged as she leafed through another book. "I would never have hired the guy."

"You mean you'd never trust anyone who'd been in prison?" I asked.

"Nope," she said.

"Don't you think some people can change?"

"No. Not criminals." Lashley's eyes glazed over and she stared into space.

"Once I met a kid who went to juvenile lock-up," I said. "He told me that being locked in a cell had scared him so much that he'd never break another law. Before he went to jail, he used to hang out with all these bad kids at school. They did drugs and stole things, and he had a feeling of power. Then he was arrested."

"Good thing," Lashley said harshly.

"Yeah. But after he got out of juvenile detention, he was different. He ignored all the kids in his old gang. He became a star basketball player and stayed home on weekends. He changed himself, but teachers still treated him like a criminal. Whenever there was trouble at school, he was always blamed. It wasn't fair. He tried so hard to change his life, but people at school didn't want to give him a second chance."

"But it was his fault in the first place, right?" Lashley said, frowning, and selecting more books from the shelf.

"Yes. But how long should he be punished? He paid his dues, right?"

Lashley tightened her eyes and puckered her mouth. She looked unsure of what to say. I was sure she had never met anyone who had been to jail.

She shook her head slowly. "Why should good things happen to bad people anyway, and bad things happen to people like my mom? Why was she paralyzed? She has always been a good person. Why her? You see greedy people get rich, and criminals turn into celebrities, but then good people like Mom have to suffer. And now . . . now she's . . ."

Lashley cut herself off and looked away because her eyes were watering. Her face reddened. I wanted to know what she was about to say. And now her mom . . . what? But I didn't ask.

"Lashley, do you believe there is some master plan for each person? Maybe everything happens for a reason, and we don't always know what that reason is."

"I don't believe that," Lashley said. "There is no good reason why my mother was paralyzed."

"Oh," I said, realizing Lashley was mad again. "I didn't mean your mom deserved her accident . . . I meant . . . maybe we don't know why things happen. Maybe there's a good side to everything, but we don't see it. Maybe . . . um . . . something like that."

"A good side?" Lashley said, gritting her teeth.

She looked at me hard and shook her head angrily. Walking up to the cashier, she said nothing more.

CHAPTER NINE

Sea Lions and Chopsticks

When the ferry returned us from Alcatraz to Pier 41, Lashley and I got off and asked Jason if we could wander around Fisherman's Wharf for a while. He gave us permission as long as we were back for the six o'clock dinner. He and his dad were going to be at camp again that night, and our group was going to make Chinatown plans.

As Jason led most of the campers back up to Fort Mason, Lashley and I sat down on the pier to catch the little bit of sun that was breaking through the gray clouds. Lined up all around us, tourists waited to ferry to Alcatraz or to take a boat tour of the bay. Relaxing and staring out at the water, we heard barking sounds from a nearby pier. Curious, we walked over to Pier 39 and were surprised by what we saw–sea lions of many sizes flopping all over the boat docks. The area had been closed off to boats to protect the animals.

Baby sea lions swam in the water and tried to leap onto the docks to rest in the sun. A huge male barked at the babies and kept them from finding space next to the adults. One little one managed to heave itself up and over the grouchy adult and to wiggle into a spot half on top of a dozing female. The giant males roared, lifting their heads high into the air, and butting others out of the way.

We stood there for a long time, watching the animals and smelling the earthy sea lion odor mixed with fish smells. Behind us was a poster that explained how the sea lions had "hauled out" onto Pier 39's docks shortly after the big 1989 San Francisco earthquake. Moved by this unusual sea lion behavior, the local Marine Mammal Center, and the people in charge of Pier 39, decided to let the mammals stay protected. More than three hundred sea lions now live on those docks.

"Look at how those big male sea lions boss all the others around," Lashley hissed, rolling her eyes. "Not too different from some obnoxious boys I've met."

"I hope you don't mean me," I said, feeling unsure with Lashley now.

Lashley blew air out through puckered lips. "No. I don't mean you. You never boss people around," she said. "Except today, when you made me go to Alcatraz with you." She tapped the top of my head with one hand.

"Hey. I didn't make you, " I yelped, rubbing my head and pretending that it hurt.

"Okay. Okay. Calm down."

"Calm down? You're accusing me of being a pushy male."

"No, I'm not. I was only kidding. And Alcatraz was neat . . . sort of. But it did give me the creeps."

"Me too, a little," I said.

"Really?" she said, looking at me with wide eyes. "You too?"

"Just looking into those solitary confinement cells gave me the shivers. I can't stop thinking about how scared I would feel if someone locked me into one. Imagine darkness dropping all around you when the iron door is shut. I'd feel as if I had disappeared, and I'd probably lose my mind."

We were quiet for a few minutes. I was staring at the water with unfocused eyes. Lashley shook her head and shoulders for a second as if the air had suddenly grown cold.

"I was thinking about how scared I'd feel surrounded by so many violent criminals," she said. "I would always be looking over my shoulder. You wouldn't know whom to trust." Lashley pulled two books out of her daypack. "I bought that prisoner book for you and your dad," she said, handing it to me. "And for me, I bought another one written by a guard's daughter."

"Hey, thanks," I said, taking the book and flipping through the pages again. "Dad will love this. Do you think we'll ever get to sleep tonight?"

"I don't know," Lashley said.

I dropped my new book into my daypack. "Hey, maybe we should do something fun now just to change gears."

"Sounds great. How about buying food? I'm hungry."

"Okay by me," I answered, always ready for another meal.

For the next few hours, Lashley and I wandered all along the wharf, buying chocolates in the Pier 39 shopping complex, watching marine creatures at Underwater World, and climbing through the tight quarters of the USS *Pampanito*, a submarine that sank five Japanese ships during World War II.

After touring the submarine, we went to the Maritime Museum, which faces the harbor. There, we read accounts of adventurous sea merchants and their brave wives, who often accompanied their husbands on whaling or trading expeditions in the Pacific. We also tried out the Morse code machines on the top level of the museum and listened to taped personal accounts of sailors.

After all the sightseeing, we were bushed. We could barely climb back up the long staircase to Fort Mason. When we shuffled in to dinner, our new gang looked up from their plates and laughed. Juan was sitting at Jason's table with most of our group, and Old Samuel sat rocking in his seat. He looked up from his dessert and waved at me. I smiled and put my tray down across from his.

"Our long lost friends, wayward explorers!" Juan said, pushing over to make room for us at the table. "We thought you might have been locked up on Alcatraz."

Lashley sat down next to Juan and started telling him what we had done all day. I sat on Lashley's other side and looked over at Jason and Samuel.

Jason was leaning back and sipping tea while Samuel began forking a big piece of apple pie into his mouth. Chewing, Samuel turned his eyes slightly upward to watch all the kids at the table. He had an engaged expression that made me think he noticed everything that went on.

"You two are looking inspired," Jason said, as Lashley and I shook out our napkins and dug into our cheese quiche. "When you've eaten you can tell us all about your adventures. But now I want to talk about our Chinatown dinner. I've called over my group to make plans. Juan, I don't want you to feel excluded. You should head over now to Don's table to hear the plans for your own group."

Juan got up and saluted us. "Friends, I'll be seeing you at the after-dinner jam." He nodded quickly at me and then looked at Lashley with raised eyebrows. "Hope you'll play something tonight, Lashley."

Lashley smiled back at him and said, "Maybe. We'll see."

Suddenly, Juan was silent, and he turned on his heels to hurry to his own table. Coming toward us, late as usual, was Peter. Dropping his tray down loudly onto the table, he sat down next to Lashley where Juan had been sitting. Lashley didn't flinch, but my stomach muscles tightened again. I just hated being in the same breathing space with Peter.

"Okay," said Jason. "Now to the Chinatown plans. First, we'll all take the streetcar to my apartment in Chinatown. Then, we'll go shopping for fresh fish and vegetables. Dad and I will cook for all of us, and you guys can help. Let's plan the menu and make sure nobody has any food allergies, or whatnot."

Somewhere in my brain I heard Jason talking, but I couldn't concentrate on what he was saying. I was too busy worrying about Peter. I could tell he was trying to get Lashley's attention, and I didn't like it.

"Dad and I love to cook Chinese food the way my mother used to make it," Jason said. "For our dinner, we're going to chop vegetables, garlic, and ginger. Some of you can fill the dumplings. I'll send two of you to buy fortune cookies, others to buy vegetables, and two more to get chopsticks from a store called the Wok Shop."

Samuel grinned. Lashley sat up and wiggled, smiling.

"Oh, please, could Eric and I buy the chopsticks?" Lashley begged Jason. "I've heard all about the Wok Shop. Please, please, please."

Peter peered at Lashley and sighed noisily. "Oh, please, please, please," he said, mocking Lashley.

Everyone noticed and stared at Peter and Lashley. There was dead silence for a second.

Slowly, Lashley turned to Peter, raised and straightened her shoulders, and crossed her arms in front of her chest. Seeing Lashley in a huff, Peter actually looked down, moved slightly away from her, and played nervously with a napkin in his hands.

I was amazed. Peter actually looked meek for a second. And afraid of Lashley.

And she looked like a mother lion about to pounce.

"If you, Peter Mooring, are mocking my enthusiasm for adventure," Lashley said slowly, "then I feel sorry for you. Your life must be as dull as watching corn grow. Or, perhaps you think you've seen it all because you live in Los Angeles, your Mecca of the United States. You would believe that only because you have never been to New Orleans."

Lashley cleared her throat. She was not finished. "Strange how some human males act just like those big, smelly, male sea lions at Pier 39."

The whole table cracked up laughing, except Peter. Samuel slapped his knee and threw his head back. Jason smiled but didn't say anything. Peter just sat still. He looked as if he didn't know what to do. I was stunned that he didn't fight back. He was probably acting polite in front of grown-ups again. He lifted his head, shrugged, rolled his eyes, and with two hands he threw bits of his shredded napkin up into the air.

More laughter from the table.

"She got you good," Old Samuel croaked, whacking his hands together and hooting again with laughter. "An' you took it like a brave sea lion!"

Everyone cracked up even louder, and then Peter actually laughed with Samuel. He threw up his palms again as if to say, "She got me." Gunter almost fell backward he was laughing so hard. Tenzin choked on his dessert and had to lean over and cough until his throat was clear.

"Hey, Eric," Jason said loudly.

"Yeah?" I said.

"Sorry guy, but I'm going to have to let Peter go with Lashley to the Wok Shop. They both just earned a shopping trip together."

"But!" I said, gulping. "Lashley and I are a team."

Lashley looked at Jason. "What? Go with a sea lion?" she said. "Jason, that wouldn't be proper. We're of different species."

Jason laughed again. "Lashley, you and Peter can manage together," he said. "You can't stick around with old friends all the time. You came here to meet other musicians. Here's your chance."

I couldn't tell what Lashley was thinking, but Peter was looking like a satisfied gorilla. Practically thumping his chest. By acting the oaf, he had just earned a big reward. Shopping with Lashley. And he had hardly opened his mouth.

I looked up just as Samuel reached over and patted my arm. He must have known what I was thinking again. He raised his eyebrows at me and swayed forward and back, forward and back. On the back of my left hand, he patted out a slow rhythm.

After telling us the rest of the plans for our Chinese dinner, Jason went up onto the dining room stage and announced that we would start an open-mike night, and that anyone who felt like playing should sign up on the players' list.

Samuel slowly hobbled onto the stage and sat down on the small wooden stool behind a microphone. Grinning as usual, he stared out above the heads of the campers. I gave him a small wave, which he noticed and acknowledged with a sideways toss of his head and a wink. Jason handed Samuel the resonator guitar, and Samuel hardly took another breath before picking the strings and rocking his chest forward and back. Jason pulled out the same banjo he had played on our first night, and the two launched into another improvised session that got everyone's attention. Campers began to move to seats closer to the stage and to stomp their feet on the floor. One by one, young musicians put their names on the players' list.

"Where's our bass?" Jason asked the audience after he and Samuel had finished the first piece. "We need a bass player. Gunter, come on up here!"

Gunter popped his head up from talking to Tenzin and pointed to himself, questioning. "Me?"

"Yes, you!" Jason said, waving Gunter up on stage.

Gunter grabbed his bass guitar and loped like an ostrich onto the stage. He started right in on the beat with Samuel and Jason, and smiled wildly as his guitar fell in with the improvised rhythm. He looked elated, and his mood made me want to go up there too. Grabbing Lashley by the arm, I got her attention.

"Hey, want to go up and play something together?" I asked, starting to stand up.

"Nah. I'm not in the mood," Lashley said, without looking at me.

"But we could do "Jammin' on the Avenue," like we did in your dad's studio," I said. "Come on."

Lashley scowled and slid a few inches away from me toward Peter. "Eric, I said I'm not in the mood."

My gut sank. Peter looked at me and grinned. At that moment I realized what was going on. Lashley was using Peter to push me away again, and I had no idea why. If I was going to play guitar that night, I thought, I was going to have to do it without her.

I looked up at Samuel onstage, and he looked back at me. Then he waved to me to join him. Without saying another word to Lashley, I walked to the stage with my guitar and climbed up to stand beside Samuel. Getting into the rhythm, I began to strum a blues in E. With that slow beat came the heavy feeling that Lashley and I were slipping far, far apart. But, I was still hanging on to any thread that we had between us.

CHAPTER TEN

Troubling Inspiration

After the open-mike night, I tossed around in my bunk bed for more than an hour. I decided to get up and take my new Alcatraz book out to the hostel living room, where I could read. Sitting up, I heard Spencer whisper something to me.

"What?" I asked him as quietly as possible. I didn't want to wake up the other guys. Spencer had a pillow over his head, which he lifted at the corner.

"You sick or something?" he asked. "You've been rolling all over the place tonight."

"Nah, I'm fine," I said. "The music gave me an adrenaline rush, and I'm not tired yet."

"Okay. That's good."

"Sorry to keep you awake, Spencer. I'm going out for a while."

Spencer mumbled something in reply, but he sounded more asleep than awake.

Holding my breath, I stepped lightly down the ladder at the end of my bunk. Somebody turned over and muttered in his sleep just as I closed the bedroom door and stepped into the lighted hallway. The air was still, and the building seemed deserted without the usual weaving of campers through the hallways. I heard the sounds of a radio turned way down. Someone must have been stationed at the reception desk.

As I walked into the living room, I saw someone's head in a high-back armchair in front of an empty fireplace. It didn't take me more than an instant to know who was there. Lashley. She couldn't sleep either, I figured.

I stopped in the doorway, deciding whether to go in or leave.

"Hi, Eric," she said, softly.

"Hi," I said, frozen in the doorway.

"Come read with me," she said in a friendly voice.

But I wasn't sure I wanted to. Lashley was so warm one minute and chilly the next that I just couldn't keep up with her moods.

Then I thought, oh, why not? I walked around the side of her chair and slumped into the couch next to it.

"What are you reading?" I asked, without looking at her directly.

Lashley showed me the front of her book, the one she had bought for herself on Alcatraz.

"Is it good?" I asked, lifting up my Alcatraz book.

"Yeah. It's good," she said. "I'm just surprised the guards and their families weren't more frightened living on Alcatraz with more than two hundred convicts. I would have been." Lashley looked back down at her book. She was avoiding my eyes too.

I began flipping through my book and reading about a prisoner who left Alcatraz and started a new life. Within three pages, I was as absorbed as Lashley in Alcatraz tales, and we were quiet for a long time.

Abruptly, Lashley broke the silence. "Hey, look at this picture," she said, leaning forward out of her chair and showing me her book. "They had a band out at Alcatraz."

I took the book and looked at the picture of a band playing for the prisoners in the dining room. Some of the prisoners were shielding their faces from the camera.

"I guess they don't like having their picture taken. They're all looking away or covering their eyes."

"Well, sure. Would you want your picture taken if you were a prisoner?"

"I guess not," I said. "Hey, what kind of guitars are those guys playing anyway?" I squinted at the page to get a good look at the instruments.

"I read in one of the books," Lashley said, "that a prisoner hid metal objects in a resonator guitar when he walked through a metal detector. Because the guitar has a metal body, it always triggered the detectors. The guards didn't bother to check inside the guitar. Knives and files circulated through the prison that way."

"Ingenious," I said, amazed what prisoners would do.

"Frightening," Lashley said, scowling at me. "Why are you always on the prisoners' side?"

"I'm not," I said, defensively. "I'm just interested in what they think up."

"They think up evil. That's what they think up!"

Here we go again, I thought. Why can't we just get along? I wondered. I changed the subject.

"Hey, what do you know?" I said, lifting Lashley's book up very close to my eyes.

"What?" Lashley reached for the book. I leaned toward her and pointed at the guitar in the picture.

"That's amazing!"

"What?" Lashley asked again.

"See that instrument?" I asked. "Ever seen it before?"

"I don't know," Lashley said. "I can hardly see it in that picture. It's so small."

"Wow, it's got to be . . ."

"Are you going to tell me what's so amazing?"

"*That . . . that* . . . is . . . Old Samuel's resonator guitar–the one he plays all the time."

"No way. How could it be?" Lashley said.

"It *is*. I would recognize it anywhere. There aren't too many of those guitars around."

"You can't be absolutely sure though."

"Yes I can. I'm sure. Trust me."

I sat back for a second, thinking about my conversation with Jason. "Remember when Jason said his teacher won the guitar in a card game? Then we found out that his teacher

was his father. So his father must have won it and . . ."

"I still don't believe it's the same guitar," Lashley said.

She leaned back in her armchair, shutting off our conversation. I couldn't see her whole face because it was hidden behind the wing of the chair, but she was irritated. Or scared.

"You don't suppose," I whispered, thinking fast, making connections. "Whoa! . . . Nah . . . it couldn't be."

"Couldn't be what?" Lashley asked sharply, leaning forward again and slapping her hand down hard against her thighs.

"Do you think that Samuel won it in a card game off some Alcatraz prisoner?"

"Ah, come on, Eric. It's late. Will you just drop it?"

"But maybe Samuel had a friend in Alcatraz."

"I doubt it. I'm sure it's just a coincidence. I don't even care," she said, taking her book back from me. "Eric, this thing about Samuel, the resonator, and Alcatraz. Aren't you just a bit obsessed? Can't you think about anything else?"

"I'm not obsessed," I said. "It's just that Samuel's cool. Have you ever met a guitarist like him? When he plays, my blood gets all jumpy. See how fast his fingers move but they're still gentle. How many people in the world can play like that?"

"It's just that you never think about anything else. Samuel and Alcatraz. Alcatraz and Samuel. Resonator and Alcatraz. And you're always staring at Samuel and ignoring the rest of us. Enough already. I'm sick of it."

"I'm sorry if you don't like him, Lashley. But I do. He's the coolest musician I've ever met, and I want to get to know him. Can't you understand that? You're a musician too."

"He's just weird, Eric. He's always looking at you and patting your arm. Why does he do that?"

"It's not weird. He just likes me. We're alike somehow. I don't know. I think we're trying to say the same things with music. He just does it a lot better than I do."

"Well, I don't like his style," Lashley said. "It's too . . . too . . . unpredictable."

Lashley stared into the empty fireplace. Her eyebrows were drawn down tightly over her eyelids, and she chewed the inside of her cheek again. Fingers tapping on the back of her book, she seemed unreachable. The gap between us was now huge.

"I'm sorry, Lash," I said quietly, getting up to go. "I didn't mean to ignore you, if that's what you say I was doing."

Lashley was still. She didn't say a word.

"Samuel is the greatest inspiration I've ever had. I can't walk away from that."

CHAPTER ELEVEN

Picking with Fingers

I had been to eat in Chinatown in Boston when my brother celebrated winning the state finals in ice hockey, but that Chinatown is nothing compared to Chinatown in San Francisco. This West Coast Chinatown has the second-largest community of Chinese outside Asia and looked to me like a foreign country. Crowded streets, back alley noodle shops, temples, laundries, and bushels and bushels of Chinese cabbage, crinkled mushrooms, and strange prickly fruits. Meat markets display whole pig heads (which was enough to turn me into a vegetarian), and discount stores with wide entrances display baskets of teas, yin-yang stickers, Chinese slippers, and plastic Buddha statues for the tourists. Spicy incense mixes with drafts of garlic and ginger to float up your nostrils. And there is even a McDonald's on the first floor of a Chinese pagoda-like building made of yellow brick and dark red roofing tiles. The word *McDonald's* is written in English and in Chinese.

Not far down the street from McDonald's, I saw a huge store devoted to ginseng. I didn't even know what ginseng was until Jason explained that Chinese people use it as a health tonic. You can buy ginseng roots, ginseng tea, ginseng pills, and ginseng hard candy. Jason told me that his mother had given him ginseng for every cold and flu and broken bone he'd ever had. She'd said it even cured teenage pimples, which made me laugh.

Walking down the streets of Chinatown, I noticed that people bustled and bumped each other without excusing themselves. I wondered if they were so used to crowded streets that a little bumping was nothing. Many of the Chinese in Chinatown didn't speak English, and lots of store signs were only in Chinese. Jason said that most of the older Chinese spoke Cantonese, which he used to speak with his mother, who had died three years earlier.

Our group of ten kids had taken a local bus from camp and then transferred to a streetcar up Mason Street to Jason's apartment at the corner of Mason and Jackson. From the flat rooftop of Jason's place, we looked out over much of the city. I spotted the tall Coit Tower; the Golden Gate Bridge; the hilly streets of multicolored, Victorian-style houses; and a web of staircases and alleys behind Chinatown homes. I could smell more garlic frying and could hear adults calling children to come in from the streets.

After drinking Jason's jasmine tea, we all set off for the market to fetch ingredients for our noodle soup and dumplings. We were assigned in pairs–Lashley and Peter, Gunter and Tenzin, Rebecca and Allison, and John and Nelson. I went off with Daniel, a quiet kid who didn't have much to say as we hunted for a fortune cookie factory in an unmarked alley. Luckily, the factory was close to the apartment, so Daniel and I were the first ones back from shopping. Daniel and Jason started a conversation in the kitchen, so I went to the den to find Samuel.

Carrying two mugs of jasmine tea from the kitchen, I placed one on the table in front of Samuel and the other in front of the armchair where I sat down. At first, I wasn't sure if Samuel knew I was there. He was humming and staring at a photograph on the wall, a photograph of a young man playing guitar.

"Is that you?" I asked him softly.

He turned to me and stared for a second, perhaps startled that I was there.

"The picture," I said, pointing to the wall. "Is that you as a young man?"

Samuel smiled, took a long breath, and patted me on the knee. He coughed and cleared his throat. For him, talking seemed to take great effort.

"No sirree," Samuel said. "That man taught me to play guitar when I was in my twenties. His name was Fingers, on account o' his fast fingers on the guitar."

"If he was your teacher, he must have been amazing. I really want to learn to play like you."

This made Samuel laugh and slap his knee. He coughed again deeply, making a hollow sound in his chest.

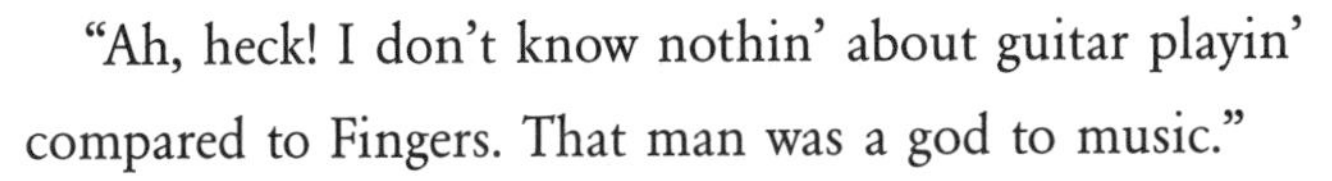

"Ah, heck! I don't know nothin' about guitar playin' compared to Fingers. That man was a god to music."

"Is he still alive?"

"Who? Fingers?" He hesitated before going on. "Nah. Fingers met his end in 1946. He was much too young to die, but his life was pretty messed up."

Samuel's mind seemed to drift off again. I couldn't tell if he had forgotten I was talking to him.

I got up for a second and stood in front of the photograph to get a better look.

"Did Fingers give you that resonator guitar, then?" I asked. "Isn't that the same one you and Jason play?"

Samuel nodded at me and gave me a wide grin. "You're pretty sharp there, boy," he said. "Fingers didn't exactly give me his guitar . . . though he would have if I'd asked for it. He was a generous guy." Samuel paused. "Nah, I won that guitar off Fingers in a card game when we was both in Alcatraz."

There it was. Just what I was wondering about after looking in Lashley's book. Samuel had been in Alcatraz.

"Did you work in Alcatraz, Samuel?" I asked, sitting back down.

"Work?" Samuel gave a short laugh. "Well, I guess you could say I worked in Alcatraz. Just livin' in there was work . . . torture . . . every day. And yeah, I worked in the prison kitchen sometimes. But, nah. I was a prisoner, son. A real prisoner from 1939 to 1955."

Nodding, I tried to swallow a tense feeling. I didn't know what to say.

"Oh," I said, hesitating. "That must have been bad."

"Well," Samuel said, coughing again. "Some of it was bad, but I deserved it. I was a no-good teenager before I got straightened out in prison."

"I can't imagine you as a prisoner."

"Yup," he said, sucking air in through his teeth. "But I got no pictures of that time. I wasn't very proud of myself back then, but I was saved."

I wasn't sure how much I could ask. "So why did you go to prison anyway?"

"Well, I didn't murder nobody, if that's what you're thinkin'," he began. "I robbed a country post office of twenty-six dollars when I was out of a job. Then I got into a fight at the first prison, so they sent me to Alcatraz, where all bad cases went."

"Oh," I whispered, wanting to know more.

"Stupid, really," he said. "Robbin' a post office is a federal offense, even if you only steal twenty-six dollars. I was real angry at the world when I did it. My mother died when I was fourteen, and my future looked bleak after that. I thought the world was unfair, and I didn't care what happened to me. I ignored all my friends because they still had mothers, and I couldn't stand the thought of that. Goin' to prison changed my whole life . . . mostly for the better."

"For the better? How?"

"On account o' that guy Fingers," he said. "You see, Fingers knew how to survive in prison. At least until his number was up. Fingers had been in and out of jails since he was a kid. He was one wild boy, but with a big heart. He kept stealin' things and givin' them to his sister, or mother, or girlfriends. Just lookin' for love, and tryin' to win it with fancy presents. Eventually, the cops stopped his stealin', and off he went to prison, again and again. He never could stay out longer than a few months. I always asked myself if maybe Fingers liked jail better than home. His family life was pretty bad."

"So how did Fingers make your life better?" I asked. I was thinking back to our tour of Alcatraz and imagining Samuel sitting in a cell by himself. I wondered if he had ever been thrown into the isolation cells.

"Fingers an' me had cells next to each other, side by side. He taught me stuff about stayin' clean in jail. We used to play cards by stickin' our hands out between the bars and puttin' the card pile in the corridor in front of us. One night I was on a roll, and I won that resonator guitar off o' Fingers. He was mighty upset, really, because his guitar meant everything to him. I told him he didn't have to give it to me, but he wanted to honor my winnin'. I decided he could give me guitar lessons instead. And that's what we did. We shared the guitar, and he taught me to play. Because I couldn't see into his cell, he drawed the finger positions for me on a piece of paper. Just learnin' to play the guitar gave me somethin' useful to do, somethin' to feel good about. I never went past ninth grade, so I had nothin' else back then."

My mind was flooded with more questions. I kept hoping the other kids would stay away all night.

"So how did you end up with the guitar?"

"Hmmm," mumbled Samuel. "That's the sad part. Fingers caught pneumonia an' he never recovered. Alcatraz was so cold and damp–I'm real surprised any of us survived. He gave me his guitar in the end. It was like having a piece of him. Poor Fingers. Never had a real happy day in his life. Me, on the other hand, with Fingers's guitar, I made myself happy. Even in 'The Hole,' I had music to think about."

"You were in 'The Hole'? In those isolation cells?"

"Yup, I was."

Remembering those cells, I clenched my teeth. "What was it like in there? Weren't you scared?"

Samuel took a long drink of tea. "You betcha I was scared. The first day I screamed and screamed for someone to let me out. I couldn't even see my hand in front of my face or nothin'. I felt like I done vanished, or something, that I had died already and gone to some dark place. I took hold of my crossed arms and rocked forward and back, forward and back against the wall for days. I was so out of my mind. I couldn't even tell if I was breathing."

"How did you survive?"

"Well, it took me days to calm down. But then I was tuckered out. Couldn't scream no more. Finally I crawled around the whole cell, touchin' the wall, an' I realized I was safe. I knew they'd bring me food. I just had to hold on to my mind. I chose a corner of the cell and stayed there most of the next two weeks. I decided to practice guitar to keep my mind settled. Pretendin' to hold my guitar, I moved my fingers up and down the neck, singin', makin' up songs, hummin'. . . I saw my guitar in my hands even though it weren't there, really. I felt like I was playin' for the whole world, and for some kind of angel or something who looked out for me even though I was so bad. I kept my mind on that guitar for fourteen days straight, an' I became really quiet inside."

Samuel drank more tea and sighed deeply.

"After that, I was a new man. When I got back to my regular cell an' saw my real guitar, I cried like a baby. What I figured out was that music had saved me. So, I decided then and there to dedicate the rest of my life to music–playin' it and teachin' it–and to this angel who listened to my music. Sometimes I like to walk up to that Grace Cathedral near here–though I'm not much of a church man–an' walk through that labyrinth they got up there. I feel like I'm singin' and breathin' inside an' saying thanks for my second life."

"What was it like getting out of prison after so long in there?" I asked, almost breathless with Samuel's story.

"When I first got out of prison, I got a day job as a cook in a Chinese restaurant. In the evenings, I played music around town or gave lessons. For a while, I still felt like a prisoner, but then I fell in love with a waitress at the restaurant. She knew I'd been in Alcatraz, but didn't care. She trusted me, an' we decided to be a family. Just the idea of a family made me feel so good, made me feel like I still had lots of time left to be a good man. When Jason was born, I was the happiest father in the world."

"Did people treat you okay when you got out of prison? Were they scared of you?"

"Well," said Samuel, closing his eyes for a second and yawning. "Some people treated me bad, but that's okay. They was just scared. I never let that bother me 'cause it's human nature to be scared o' what you don't know. One day I saw the cop who put me in jail, an' I told him I'd probably be dead by now if he hadn't put a stop to my bad ways."

"Amazing," I said, sitting back to think about Samuel's story.

Samuel finished his tea and rested his head back against his chair, eyes closed, humming. I didn't want to disturb him but I wanted to hear more.

"Samuel?"

"Mmmm." He didn't lift his head or open his eyes.

"Can you answer one more question?"

"Boy, you are full of questions, ain't you? Well, that's a good thing. Jason's the same. You learn about the world that way. Okay, one more question."

"Samuel, I read in a book that an Alcatraz prisoner hid knives and tools inside a resonator guitar to get through metal detectors. Is that true? Did you do that?"

"Eric, you are a wise, wise boy," Samuel said. "Yeah, that did happen . . . but it wasn't me who did it. It was a guy named 'Pickax'–on account o' he could pick almost any lock–an' he was fast when he slipped those things into my guitar. But, once I got caught, and I took the fall. Life got pretty bad for me after that."

"Is that why they put you in 'The Hole?'"

"Yup, that's the reason," he said, sleepily. "And now Old Samuel needs a little rest, Eric. You got me rememberin' a lot of my life, and I need to doze. We'll have time to talk again later."

Before I could say anything more, Samuel was snoring lightly, his head back and his mouth open. I watched him for a minute, thinking about the life he'd lived. Then I heard noises from the other rooms. The group was coming back in from Chinatown shopping.

CHAPTER TWELVE

Trembling Labyrinth

Standing in Jason's living room, I heard clomping up the outer staircase to the apartment. Loud and laughing, Lashley and Peter came bursting through the kitchen door. They flung plastic shopping bags through the air and onto the kitchen counter, and they looked happy–something I never would have expected. Peter leaned in to Lashley and whispered in her ear, which made her squeal in hysterics. The other kids soon crowded through the door, and filled the kitchen with bodies. I hung back in the living room and could barely see the top of Lashley's head as she leaned her backside on the counter and swung out her feet, giggling.

"Hey, Lash," I called from the living room. She didn't look up. I don't think she heard me above the noise. The kids were telling Jason about their adventures in Chinatown, and Peter moved closer to Lashley. They were talking, head to head. After listening to Samuel's story, I just wasn't in the mood to go into the kitchen. But, I wanted to tell Lashley what I had just heard.

"Lashley!" I repeated, waving to get her attention. She looked up, and I signaled at her anxiously to come into the living room. “I have something to tell you,” I mouthed without sound.

She held up her open palm, telling me to wait, that she’d talk to me in a second. She pointed at her shopping bags on the counter, showing me she had to empty them first before coming into the living room. She looked away again, still resting against the counter, not touching her shopping bags. Peter glanced at me, raised his eyebrows, and then turned back to talk to Lashley. I stood in the living room, frozen. Uncomfortable. Wondering which way to move. Into the kitchen to join the others? Into the den to wake up Samuel?

Suddenly, I wondered if I should tell Lashley, or anyone, about Samuel’s past. He hadn’t told me to keep his story a secret, nor did he give me permission to repeat it. At that moment, I realized I didn’t want to break Samuel’s confidence in me. But I was confused. There I was trying to become friends with an ex-convict while the close friend I thought I had was suddenly giggling and sharing secrets with the camp bully.

I raced into the bathroom before Lashley could come ask me what I wanted. I leaned over for a drink of water from the sink faucet.

Standing up and looking at myself in the mirror, I breathed in slowly. What was going on? I asked myself. What was happening to Lashley? And to me? Why was Lashley pulling away from me and having fun with the same guy we had been trying to avoid a few days ago?

I really needed to talk to someone. Samuel was asleep, and Jason was busy. Lashley was with Peter, and Juan and Spencer were somewhere in Chinatown with their own camp group. So, who was left? What was I going to do?

I wanted to get out of the bathroom unnoticed, but how? Looking out the bathroom window, I spotted a fire escape that I could easily reach. Without planning where I was going, I lifted the window and screen, and stretched my body out through the frame and onto the metal steps. Closing the screen and window as best I could, I made my way down quickly and jumped to the street.

As soon as I hit the ground, I took off running up Mason Street and out of sight. The street was steep, which slowed me down, but I didn't see anyone following me. Near the top of the hill, I slowed to a walk and found myself in front of the large, deluxe Fairmont Hotel.

I stood still for a moment, wondering where to go next, wondering why I was running. Sitting down on the curb in front of the hotel, I caught my breath and watched a stream of people dressed in evening clothes exit the hotel and ask one of the doormen to call them a cab. Where were they going? I asked myself. What was everyone else doing while I sat there on an unfamiliar curb, feeling lonely? I dropped my head onto my knees and closed my eyes. I began to sway slightly, hearing the echo of a song Samuel had played.

"Are you okay?" a voice said to me.

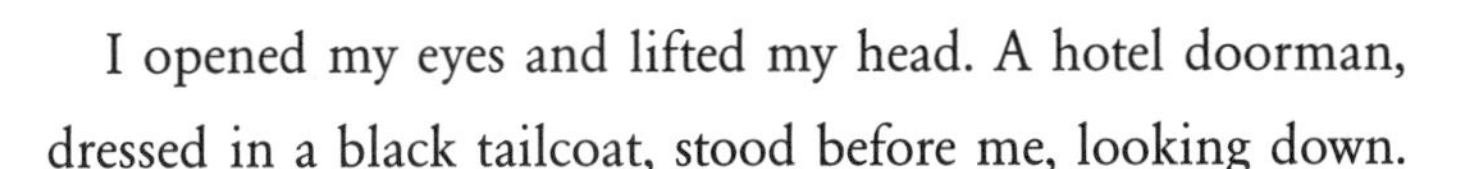

I opened my eyes and lifted my head. A hotel doorman, dressed in a black tailcoat, stood before me, looking down.

"Oh, yeah, I'm fine. I was just out of breath from running up the hill."

"A steep one, isn't it," the man said, looking down the Mason Street incline.

"Sure is."

"You a runner?" the doorman asked, his expression open and friendly.

"Nah," I said, not knowing what else to say. "Uh, I just felt like running up here . . ."

"Good challenge," he said, nodding at me. "But . . . well . . . I can't let you sit on this curb too long, buddy. You might scare away the hotel guests."

Me? Scare away hotel guests? I wondered.

"Uh . . . actually . . . I am looking for Grace Cathedral," I said, not sure why. "A friend told me about it. He said it was somewhere up here."

The doorman pointed at a building one block away. "That's Grace Cathedral right over there."

"Uh. Oh . . . thanks," I said. "I was too busy panting to look." I noticed the evening darkness and wondered what time it was.

The doorman shrugged and chuckled as he started to walk away. "Go check it out. It's beautiful. And they have a labyrinth over there too."

"That's just what I was planning to do," I lied. "Thanks."

The truth is, I didn't even know exactly what a labyrinth was, but I was curious to find out. I stood up and walked the block past a small, grassy park to Grace Cathedral. I noticed a sign showing an outdoor and an indoor labyrinth. They looked kind of like mazes except without the dead ends. The air was growing chilly, so I decided to go into the cathedral.

Stepping inside, my whole body instantly grew quiet in the still of the church. Just a handful of whispering people wandered around looking at the statues, murals, and stained-glass windows. For a moment I felt as if I had just walked through a time warp to another century in the past.

Reading a sign inside the cathedral, I learned the meaning of the labyrinth and how to walk through it. The sign explained that by taking the winding path you could discover a shared spiritual journey. Why not? I said to myself. Better than trying to get Lashley's attention. I took off my shoes and put them under a wooden chair, and then I just followed the single path marked on the rug. I wasn't sure if I was supposed to think about anything special, and I felt a little bit silly wandering there. But nobody really paid any attention to me, so I kept going.

Only one other person was in the labyrinth that evening, and he was sitting still in one of the petals of the flower-shaped center space. The sign had said that once you reach the middle you choose a spot and sit until you're ready to walk out. After winding slowly, I reached the inner area. I chose a space across from the man, and sat down to relax. Soon, the man got up, nodded at me, and walked out the way I had come in. After that, I was alone in the labyrinth, and I saw only a few other people at the far end of the cathedral.

An organist began playing somewhere, and long notes floated up from the organ pipes and filled the building. I sensed something unseen around me, but I didn't really know what it was. Maybe that's what Samuel liked about the labyrinth, I thought–the invisible something that felt like friendship.

Sitting quietly, I had the chance to let my mind think back to Samuel and to Lashley. One thought was bothering me. I wanted to spend more time with Samuel and to learn to play like him, but I knew that Lashley would ignore me even more if I did. She didn't like Samuel, and she would really hate him if she knew he had been a prisoner. She was clear on how she felt about criminals. She wasn't going to give them a break.

As these thoughts came up in my mind, I remembered something that Samuel had said, and then something similar that Lashley had said. Suddenly, I saw a connection between the two. How could I have missed it before? In a flash I knew what was the matter with Lashley, what was making her so moody and angry.

I had to talk to her. It all made sense. I had to get back to Lashley and help her. And maybe Samuel could help her too.

Just as I was about to get up, I heard a terrible crashing noise at the back of the cathedral. Then a woman's scream and the high-pitched sound of breaking glass pierced the air. Perhaps someone had thrown a rock at one of the windows, I thought. Suddenly the ground shook under me, and I slapped my palms to the floor, trying to steady myself. From the altar, four people came running toward me.

"Run, boy," somebody shouted. "It's a quake. Get somewhere safe."

"What?!" I screamed, confused. "What's happening?"

A man ran across the labyrinth and grabbed me by the arm, pulling me up.

"An earthquake, son, an earthquake."

The man had me up on my feet and was dragging me forward. "We've got to get somewhere safe."

"Wait," I shouted. "My shoes." I scrambled over to my shoes, yanking the man with me. Then I felt another person grab my other arm, and I was practically lifted through the air. I had my shoes by the laces as we ran to the exit. More people were running behind us, and we all pushed through the heavy doors of the church. Outside, everything was jumbled up, and I couldn't tell what was going on. People were running in every direction, and sirens were going off across the city. Flashing lights and cracking sounds confused me, and then, suddenly, the street and building lights went out. We ran in darkness. Voices came out of nowhere. Somebody was still holding on to me and pulling me away from the cathedral. I heard an electrical wire pop, and then sirens got louder and closer. I was running . . . running . . . tripping, and scurrying behind the man who pulled me. Finally we came to a stop, and I squatted on the ground. Slowly, I caught my breath and put my shoes back on. The soles of my feet burned and my socks were torn from running on the pavement.

After some time crouched down, I realized I was surrounded by the people who had led me out of the cathedral. The ground had stopped shaking, and I could hear the voices around me. Somebody had a mini flashlight and was pointing it in people's faces.

"Okay. It's over now," a man said. "I don't think it was a bad one."

"Just a tremor, really," someone else said.

"I heard windows breaking," a third voice said. "There must be some building damage."

"Let's hope that's all there was," the first man said.

"The power's out for while. Maybe the hotel will start up a generator."

Listening to the voices above me calming down, I realized I could stand up safely.

"Where are your parents, son?" somebody asked me.

I looked up and saw the same hotel doorman in a tailcoat leaning over me. He stuck out his hand for me to grab, and I pulled myself up.

"Ah . . . they're not here. I'm in camp." My voice sounded strange, garbled, as if I had thick cotton under my tongue.

"Camp?" the doorman asked. "Who's in charge of you then?"

The people who had run out of the cathedral were looking at me. I turned to them.

"Thanks for pulling me out," I said to the man I thought had grabbed my arm. "Was it you?"

A short man with glasses looked at me and smiled. He muttered something I could not hear and then said something to the hotel doorman.

"What's your name, kid?" the doorman asked me.

"Eric," I said. "Eric Wieman."

"Well, Eric, aren't you here with somebody? Where is your camp?"

Just then, I thought of Samuel and Lashley again. Where were they? Were they safe? I had to get to them right away. I had to run down the hill.

"The camp," I said, pointing down the hill. "The camp is down there. I've got to go. I've got to find my friends."

And before the doorman could stop me, I took off in a run toward Jason's apartment.

"Hey, Eric! Don't run away. It may not be safe in the streets!" the doorman shouted.

"I'll be okay," I shouted back, as if I knew what to do after an earthquake. Actually, I had no idea what I was doing. I had no idea of the danger. I just had to find Samuel and Lashley.

CHAPTER THIRTEEN

Slow Stepping

When I got back to the door at Jason's apartment, I stopped short at the sight in front of me. A streetlight had toppled over and landed right in front of the building entrance, blocking it. The facade of the building had partially collapsed, and debris and broken glass covered the streetlight and the sidewalk.

How could Jason and everybody get out? I asked myself. Were they inside? I called for Jason and Lashley, but I heard nothing from inside.

"I saw them go out a while ago," someone said to me through the darkness. "Before the quake."

I spun around and saw an Asian American woman in the street. Behind her was a cluster of people looking at the buildings along Jackson Street.

"Who?" I asked the woman. "How many of them?"

"Well, let's see," the woman said, drawing her eyebrows together. "I saw Jason and several kids. I can't say how many. Maybe seven or eight. I'm not sure."

"You said they went out BEFORE the quake?" I asked in a shaky voice.

"Yes. I was looking out my kitchen window. I heard the group of them calling for something. I thought they might have lost a dog. All that happened before the quake."

"Was Old Samuel with them?" I asked.

"I don't think so," she said. "I didn't see him."

I looked up at the windows of Jason's apartment. "He could still be in there, then," I said.

"I don't know," the woman said. She turned around to pick up a whining little girl. "It's okay, sweetie. Everything's okay. Our house is fine. It's dark, but we're fine."

The woman patted the little girl on the back, and the child rested her head on the woman's shoulder.

"I've got to go help Samuel," I said aloud.

The woman looked at me, worried. "Son, it's too dark. You shouldn't go in there until we know the area is safe. Someone is checking the buildings now."

I nodded at the woman and thanked her for her concern. She went back to her group across the street. Looking up again at the windows, I called for Samuel. Then I walked up Jackson Street and turned right at Mason to yell up into the side windows. No reply. Maybe they were all out. Maybe they were safe.

But what if they're not? I thought. And it's my fault they had to go looking for me. I decided to find a way in . . . and then I remembered the fire escape. I looked up and realized I'd have to climb the side of the building until I could reach the bottom of the fire escape. I spotted a drainpipe. Easy.

Finding hand-and-footholds where the drainpipe was fastened to the building, I yanked myself up until the fingers of my right hand stretched over to the fire escape. Balancing on my toes, I extended both hands to the fire escape and then pulled my legs over and up to it. Swiftly I planted my feet on the first step, and then I climbed the metal stairs to the bathroom window where I had escaped. Nobody had touched it. It was still open enough that I could put my hands in and under the window frame. I lifted up the window and the screen and carefully crawled into the bathroom. Jumping down onto the floor, I called out to Samuel. I heard nothing.

Walking down the darkened hallway, I couldn't tell if anyone was there. "Samuel?" I called out softly, not wanting to scare him. No answer. I headed toward the small den where we had sat earlier. Seeing nothing but the vaguest outline of furniture, I felt my way through the rooms. The darkness felt like a tunnel through the earth.

Then I heard snoring.

"Samuel?" I whispered. "Is that you?"

More snoring.

Hands out in front of me, taking baby steps, I approached the source of the sound. My knee bumped something hard. Samuel's knee. He made a loud sound like HARUMPH! as he awoke.

"Samuel, it's me. Eric."

"Huh? Harumph. Who's there?" he called in a hollow, faraway voice.

Kneeling down next to him, I placed my hand on his knee. "It's me, Eric."

"Oh, Eric," he said, patting my hand. "Why's it so dark?"

"There's been a small earthquake, Samuel. The city lost power."

"Earthquake? Is everyone okay?"

"I don't know, Samuel. Have you been asleep all this time?"

"Must have been."

"Do you have a flashlight?" I asked.

"Yup. In the closet there. Feel your way over," Samuel said, placing his hand on my face and turning my head to look behind me. I couldn't see anything. "There's a big flashlight on the middle shelf. See if you can get it."

I crawled on the floor until my shoulder bumped into the opened closet door. Standing up and patting my hand around the shelves, I touched small boxes, jars, buttons, and then the flashlight. Turning it on, I backed out of the closet and flashed it at Samuel's feet. I walked back to his side, sat on the floor, and opened the flashlight into a standing lantern. I could now see Samuel's face.

"What time is it, Eric?"

"I don't know. I don't have a watch. Where did everybody go?"

"Last thing I remember was Jason tellin' me they had to look for you," Samuel said, trying to stand up.

I pressed Samuel's knee with my hand. "Don't get up, Samuel. I'm not sure we can go anywhere. The front door is blocked."

"Where were you, son? Why were they looking for you?"

I was embarrassed to tell him, but I did anyway. "It's a long story. My friend Lashley and I haven't been getting along that well lately. I don't know why. We're just interested in different things now, I guess. I was hurt and wanted to run away. I found that labyrinth you told me about."

"Good place to think, ain't it?" Samuel said.

"Sure is. But then the earthquake started and some men dragged me out of the cathedral really fast."

Samuel was quiet for a minute.

"Eric, I know it's that boy Peter who's botherin' you. Right? You just got to let him be. And if your friend Lashley likes him, you got to let her be too. You can't force people to like each other or not like each other. You just have to accept them as they are if they don't want to change, or let 'em go."

"Yeah. I guess you're right, Samuel. But there's more to it than that. It's Lashley–she doesn't trust you. And if she finds out you've been a prisoner, she'll never even try to get to know you."

"That's okay, Eric. Some trust me. Some don't. Like Mrs. Alvarez at camp. She don't trust me neither. But that's okay. Others do. Give it some time."

"I doubt time will help. If you and I stay friends, Lashley will probably drop me altogether."

"Don't assume nothin', Eric. You never know. Now. We got to find Jason and the kids," Samuel said, sitting forward.

"Yeah. I know," I said. "But, the only way out is by the fire escape. Do you have any candles we can use to light the hallway and bathroom?"

"In the kitchen. The cupboard above the icebox."

With the flashlight, I found my way to the kitchen. Shining the light around the room, I saw counters covered with chopped vegetables, uncooked noodles, flour, and jars of spices. They must have left all the cooking, I thought, and gone out to look for me. I opened the cupboard above the refrigerator and grabbed candles and matches. After setting up a few candles in holders in the living room, I walked back through the flickering light into the den. The silence in the apartment made me breathe quietly.

"I think we should get out of here until we know the building is safe," I said.

"Did you find Jason yet?" Samuel asked, confused.

"We'll find him, Samuel," I said. "If I set everything up, do you think you can climb out the bathroom window and down the fire escape? It may not be easy, but I can lower the fire escape to the ground."

"Well, I can try," Samuel said, slapping his knees. "I've done harder things in my life than climbing down a fire escape."

"I'm sure you have, Samuel." I laughed. "Okay, follow me to the bathroom."

Samuel and I walked arm in arm to the bathroom, and I helped him climb very slowly through the window and onto the fire escape. I held my breath for a second as he grasped onto a metal railing and pulled himself up to standing. He was much stronger and more limber than I had expected, but I was still afraid he would stumble.

"Great job!" I called through the open window. "Now, wait there one second, Samuel. I have to blow out the candles."

I raced back into the living room and blew out the candles. Stopping suddenly, I realized we had left the resonator guitar. I hurried into the den, found the guitar in its case next to the sofa, grabbed it, and pulled the photograph of Fingers off the wall. Breathing quickly, my chest aching with nervousness, I rushed back to the bathroom window.

"Samuel, we have to take the guitar just in case we can't come back in for a while."

I heard Samuel laugh as I climbed out the window. Squeezing myself and the guitar into the small space next to Samuel, I gently pushed him behind me so I could go down first. I wanted to steady him from below if he faltered.

"Okay, Samuel. Easy does it. I'm going to lower the fire escape to the ground, and then you can follow me closely. I'll go first and help you down. Then I'll climb back up for the guitar."

Teeny step by teeny step, Samuel and I climbed backward down the fire escape. At one point, he stumbled, but my hand was on his hip helping him back into balance. As soon as he reached the ground, I asked him to stay put and wait for me as I climbed up for the guitar. My muscles felt strong and full as I raced back up the ladder.

"Dad!" I heard someone call out.

From the fire escape I shone the flashlight below and saw Jason and Juan. Jason ran to Samuel and hugged him strongly. Juan waved up at me.

"Yo, bro! What's the haps up there, man?" Juan shouted to me.

"Dad! How'd you get out?" Jason asked.

"Up here, Jason!" I yelled, grabbing the guitar and photograph and making my way back down.

"Careful, Eric," Jason shouted up to me. "Go slowly."

"Hey, man. Take it easy," Juan said, putting his arms out as if to catch me when I fell.

Guitar and flashlight in one hand, and photograph between my teeth, I cautiously made it down to the ground. Jason looked at me and sighed heavily before giving me a tight hug.

Juan slapped me on the back and said, "All right, dude!"

"You're all okay," Jason said to Juan, Samuel, and me. He sighed noisily. "We were so worried about you guys."

"We're fine," I said, catching my breath. "I just wanted to get him out of there. And the guitar!"

"Thank you, Eric," said Jason, looking me straight in the eye. "I'm grateful."

I tossed my head to the side and looked at Juan.

"Juan, how did you get here? Weren't you with your own group?"

Juan hesitated for a second. Jason touched his arm and nodded at him approvingly.

"It's okay, Juan," Jason said. "Your heart was in the right place."

"Soon as that quake hit, I got to thinking, where are my new friends?" Juan said. "They might get scared in this quake. I snuck away from my group to look for you guys. Jason found me just as I was getting here."

I swung my arm around and dropped it on Juan's shoulders.

"We're both a bit crazy, aren't we?" Juan asked, smiling.

I didn't have to say anything.

"Let's get in the van," Jason said.

Juan helped Samuel into the van, and I pulled Jason aside for a second. Grinning at him, I said, "Samuel was asleep, you know. The whole time. He had no idea what had happened."

"That's my dad," Jason chuckled. "He can sleep through anything."

I raised my eyebrows at Jason. "He must have learned that on Broadway, huh?" I whispered.

Jason's mouth dropped open, his eyebrows went up, and he looked at me in surprise. "He told you?"

I nodded my head. "Actually, I guessed. I saw a photo of his resonator in a book about Alcatraz, and then your door says

'Broadway' on it. The two were easy to put together. While you were in the kitchen this afternoon, Samuel told me all about Alcatraz."

Jason put his arm around my shoulder and pulled me into him. "You're one interesting kid, Eric. I'm glad I met you."

My face was hot with embarrassment.

"Where are Lashley and the others, Jason?" I asked sheepishly. "Is everyone okay?"

"They're fine. We were out looking for you in Chinatown when the tremor started," he said.

"Sorry," I said quietly.

"Luckily it was minor, and we were near my cousin's house, so we all went there. I tried to call Dad but the phone lines were dead. When everything stopped shaking, I borrowed my cousin's minivan and drove the kids back to camp. The neighborhoods looked okay . . . building damage and downed telephone poles."

"That's good," I said. "I guess I need to apologize to the group, don't I?"

Jason sighed and lifted his shoulders. "That's up to you, Eric. And when you're ready, maybe you can tell me what happened, why you ran away."

I didn't know what to say, so I just looked at Jason and said, "There isn't anything to tell, really. Samuel and I talked about it, and things are cool now."

Jason shrugged. "My dad's pretty smart about people, Eric. You can take his advice."

I nodded, and we walked to the van. I got into the back, and Jason spoke softly to Old Samuel.

"Dad, we're going to head back to Fort Mason now to spend a few nights with the kids. Our building is fine, but the power is out. Fort Mason has power, so we're better off there anyway. The kids really want us to stay with them. We'll have a party."

Samuel laughed and flashed me a cheery grin. "Hey, Eric! Good time to teach you to play the resonator."

I inhaled sharply with excitement and smiled at the three of them.

"All right!" I said to Old Samuel.

Not a bad way to end a complicated day.

CHAPTER FOURTEEN

Wild-Eyed Blues

When Jason, Juan, Samuel, and I finally reached Fort Mason that night, most of the camp kids were sitting around the dining room playing guitar or talking excitedly about the tremor that had shaken the city. Besides the blackout and building damage, nothing much had happened, but the kids were all wild eyed and noisy as if life had just started to sizzle. Kids who hadn't talked to each other the day before began playing guitar and joking around with each other after the earthquake.

The small quake was definitely the trigger for me to realize that running away had been a bad way to solve my problems with Lashley. Standing in the dining room entrance, I was relieved to be back with my friends. Juan, Samuel, and Jason joined the campers, but I stood still for a second, looking out the big picture window. I was calmed again by the trees illuminated by floodlights, trees standing solidly in an unmoving bay fog.

"Eric!" Lashley shouted, racing toward me. Nervous and electrified, she threw her arms around me and hugged me with force.

"Oh, Eric, I'm so sorry. I know you ran away because of me, and I feel terrible. I was worried we wouldn't find you or that you were hurt. I'm so glad you're here . . ."

She dropped her head on my shoulder for a second and then lifted it off to smile at me. I was startled and pulled a step away to look at her.

"I'm sorry too, Lash. I'm sorry I was so dense. If only I had known what was bothering you, I might have understood your moods."

Lashley looked at me blankly. "My moods?" she asked.

"Well, I didn't realize your mother was sick. I finally figured it out, though, after talking to Samuel. Sorry it took me so long."

"Huh?" Lashley gasped, frowning at me and stepping backward. "My mother is sick?"

My stomach muscles tightened. Was Lashley going to get mad again? Maybe she didn't want me to know.

"Well . . . I was talking to Samuel . . . and he said his mother died when he was fourteen . . . and he said he didn't care about the future after that, and he ignored all his friends and . . . so I thought that your mother must be sick. Remember when you started to say something about your mother and then you stopped? I thought . . . but . . . but . . . she's not sick?"

"Not that I know of," Lashley said, drawing down her eyebrows and cocking her head to one side. "You thought my mother was sick?"

My embarrassment choked me. "Um . . . well . . . I guess I thought that's why you were ignoring me and becoming friends with Peter, and why you didn't want to get to know Samuel or talk about your future, and why you didn't want to go to Alcatraz. Or, something like that . . . ah, never mind."

I had never felt so foolish, and I had no idea what to say next. I stood stiffly and wished Juan would come up and interrupt us.

Lashley looked at me for a long time and then threw her arms around me again, even tighter than the first time.

"Eric, you are the nicest guy I know," she whispered in my ear. "I'm sorry I haven't been . . . kind or whatever. . . . It's just so hard to explain."

I drew myself out of her arms a second time. "Well, you don't have to explain if you don't want to."

The conversation was making me uneasy. "Maybe we should go sit down," I said.

"No. I want to explain . . . but I feel funny telling you."

"Telling me what?"

"Well, you're probably not going to understand." Lashley kicked the toes of her shoes together.

"Try me."

"Okay . . . well . . . this may sound funny to you, but . . . well . . . here goes," Lashley said. "On our way out here, my dad announced to me–my mom already knew–that he was going to have to close down his recording studio."

"Why?" I asked.

"It's really weird. Dad said some guy scammed him in a deal, and Dad lost a lot of money. The guy invented a production company and fooled Dad into some joint plan. So far, the guy has gotten away with Dad's money, but we hired a lawyer. Dad says we're going to nail the guy, but it takes time. It just makes me so angry that someone tricked my dad."

"Man, that's so . . . I don't know . . . unbelievable." I shook my head. "So that's why you got mad every time I mentioned criminals."

Lashley nodded her head. "And because of this creep, we have to sell the studio to pay off debts."

"But, you're not going to starve or anything, right?" I asked. "I mean, your dad still has money, doesn't he?"

Lashley hesitated. "I feel strange saying this to *you* . . . I know your family doesn't have much money and all . . . but I am scared of being poor," Lashley admitted, her eyes watering, and her face growing red and blotchy.

"Poor! You're far from poor. With a house like yours and that fancy school . . . ?"

"Shh," Lashley pleaded. "That's just it. We may have to sell our house too, and I may have to switch schools."

"Welcome to the middle class, Lash. It ain't luxury, but we manage."

Lashley looked at the ground. She wasn't kidding; she really felt scared. Her shoulders slumped forward.

"Dad and I talked about music being a risky career financially."

"Risky career? Come on, Lash. We all know we don't do this for the money. We do it because it's in our blood."

Lashley sighed heavily and dropped her chin onto her chest. "Eric, you're stronger than I am, and you're not afraid."

"Not afraid? Are you kidding? I'm always afraid . . . but that doesn't stop me. If it did, I never would have gone to New Orleans or come to San Francisco. I would never have taken up music. Lash, I don't worry much about my future. I just try to get to the next stage. That's hard enough."

"But what if we can't make a living as musicians?" Lashley asked.

I shook my head in disbelief. "We'll figure that out when the time comes. Lashley, your problem is that you have never had to take a risk."

"I know." Her eyes watered.

"And you're good at everything, so you don't know what to do with a tough challenge."

She nodded her head and started to cry.

"Don't worry about being poor until you're poor. And don't worry about failing at music until you fail."

"That's not so easy. . . ." She wiped her nose and eyes with a tissue from her pocket.

"Lashley, my family has failed at a lot of things. And, we've been poor, really poor. But we just keep going. And think about

Juan. He has harder times than I do. You don't see him crying."

"But I'm afraid, Eric . . ."

"Of what?"

Lashley held back. Then she sighed loudly. "Of never making it in anything."

"We're all afraid of that."

"And my dad says that it takes money to make money . . ."

"Well, your dad may be right, but he's always had money. I mean, money is great and all, but do you really want to quit music just to make money?"

Lashley was silent. I could tell she wanted to say something else, though.

"What?" I asked.

"If we sell our house, and I go to a new school . . . then . . . uh . . ."

"Then what? You'll live in a smaller house and go to a public school. So what?"

"But, my friends . . ."

"What about them?"

She was stalling. Something else was bugging her.

"What if they won't call me anymore?"

"You mean you have friends who would drop you just because you move to a smaller house and go to public school?"

"Maybe."

"That's what you've been so worried about all this time?"

She nodded, blushing. Her face was streaked with tears.

"And you kept this from me because . . ."

She didn't answer.

"Lashley, who needs friends that shallow? You've always got Ben and Juan and me. Do you think we care about your big house?"

She shrugged.

"Nooooo!" I said loudly.

I patted her on the back.

"Thanks," she said quietly, wiping her eyes on her T-shirt. Her tissue was shredded in her hands.

"So," I said suddenly. "How about forgetting all this and joining in with the music making? They look like they're having fun over there."

Lashley sighed and smiled at me. "We're making up earthquake songs," she said.

"Earthquake songs?" I laughed. "Hey, I could make up one of those."

Lashley wiped her face again and started to walk toward the stage. She stopped and looked at me intensely.

"I wanted to tell you something else," she said.

"Yeah?"

Her face grew serious.

"You may not believe me, but Peter Mooring is a good guy after all," she said.

"Uh, okay," I answered, unconvinced but not wanting to squabble.

"No, I mean it. He really isn't a bully. He said he went along with Jordan last year because he was afraid of him. He didn't dare break away."

"Hmmm," I said, doubtful, looking across the dining room to see Peter jamming with another kid I didn't know.

"I'm serious. I believe him," Lashley said. "He said he was relieved that Jordan was kicked out of camp."

"So why has he acted like such a jerk all this time?"

"I don't know. I think he was trying to make new friends and didn't know how," she said. "But he stopped being obnoxious. He even apologized to me when we were in Chinatown. He's really funny too."

"Hmmm," I grunted again.

She paused and looked at me with still eyes. "Eric, we ALL need a second chance, you know?"

I smiled. "Okay, Lash. You got me there," I said. "But can he play bass to our lead? Our band really can't handle a third soloist."

CHAPTER FIFTEEN

Samuel's Touch

The night of the earthquake marked about the middle of the camp session, and for the next week I woke up with a sensation of jelly beans jumping in my stomach. I was excited. I had three more weeks of camp, and things were looking up. Lashley and I were friends again—without all that confusion and weirdness between us—and I was learning so much from Samuel. Finally camp was everything I had dreamed it would be.

One night after dinner, Samuel suggested I invite Lashley to join us in the living room to learn some alternate tuning on the guitar. I talked to Lashley, and she was hesitant. She didn't say she would come, but she didn't say no either. I didn't push it. I told her to do whatever she wanted.

So, I was surprised when she walked into the living room.

"Samuel," I said as Lashley walked up to us. "Did I ever tell you that Lashley and I wrote and recorded a song together last winter?"

From his chair, Samuel smiled at Lashley and raised his hand gently to catch hers and lead her to the couch. I was afraid Lashley wouldn't take Samuel's hand, but something about her suddenly turned soft and accepting. It must have been Samuel's gaze that did it. Lashley grasped his hand and walked to the couch and sat down.

"Did I tell you that, Samuel?" I asked again.

Samuel was still smiling at Lashley. And to my amazement, she smiled back. He squeezed her hand sweetly, and she kept watching him.

"No, Eric," Old Samuel said, releasing Lashley's hand. "You never told me that. Play it for me?"

Lashley shook her head. I looked at her and willed her to change her mind. Samuel reached over and patted Lashley's knee.

"Young musicians are often shy around old geezers like me," Samuel said, laughing a deep, dry laugh. "They must think I'm too old to understand new music."

Lashley's mouth dropped open. "No, it's not that," she said haltingly. "It's just . . ."

"Dear," Samuel said to Lashley, "you don't have to play for me. Your buddy here, Eric, he just likes to strut his stuff."

Lashley looked at me and cracked up laughing. "Just like those smelly sea lions, right?" Lashley joked with Samuel.

"That's right," Samuel said. "Young men are hopeless show-offs."

"Hey," I said, whacking the couch with my right hand. "I'm not a show–"

"Okay," Lashley said in the sparkly voice I remembered from New Orleans. "Let's do it, Eric. Let's play it for him."

And before she could change her mind, I handed Lashley my guitar, and I took Samuel's. We tuned up together and started in on "Jammin' on the Avenue." I picked the beginning, and Lashley backed me up, rocking and bouncing on the couch. We jumped into the song, and together we sang, smiling and laughing the way we did in New Orleans when we thought up the lyrics. Samuel slapped out our beat with his hands on his knees.

"Good beat," he said, his eyes opening wide with energy. "Good song!"

Lashley and I kept playing, becoming lighter and lighter with every note.

The toughest thing about going to camp last summer, besides all that trouble between Lashley and me, was saying good-bye to Samuel. He felt like such a part of me by the end of the summer that I didn't know how I was going to function without him. And the things he taught me . . . nobody but a musician would understand the size of the gift Old Samuel gave me. I never knew how important a music teacher could be.

"Now listen, son," Samuel said to me one evening near the end of camp.

We were sitting together on the living room couch again, playing a new song.

"I got lots more to teach you, Eric."

Already sad knowing that I would have to leave camp and Samuel in a few days, I held back from talking. I didn't want to think about leaving.

"We could work night and day and day and night until the end of camp, but that still don't give us enough time to cover everythin'," Samuel said, looking sad.

I forced myself to reply. I wanted to tell Samuel what a great teacher he was.

"I know, Samuel," I said. "And I'm grateful that you've taken all this time with me. I never imagined I would find a teacher like you."

Samuel put out his hand as if to stop me from saying anything more.

"What I'm tryin' to tell you, son, is that Jason and me have been talkin'."

"About what?" I asked.

"About you, son, about you," Old Samuel said. He put his guitar on his lap and placed both hands on my shoulders. "We set things up with Quickfinger so's you'll get a scholarship again next summer. Okay with you?"

For a moment, I couldn't speak. I just looked Samuel in the eyes.

"I don't know what to say, Samuel."

"Nothin'. Don't say nothin'," he replied.

"Samuel, I . . ." My words were caught behind my tongue.

"Nope," he said. "Don't say nothin,' son."

I nodded at him. I reached up to my shoulder and put my hand on his.

"And another thing!" Samuel now reached down to his resonator and ran his fingers over the curve of the guitar body. "I want you to keep playin' what I taught ya."

"I will, Samuel. I will."

"Yeah, but you need a resonator, son. You take this sweet guitar back home with you. It don't do me no good here no more 'cause you're its main player now. Jason and me, we got more guitars here than we can play. We both want you to have the resonator."

"No, Samuel," I said. "This guitar is tied to you. I can't take it."

"Yes, you can, if I says so. The guitar is tied to you now, Eric, an' you're tied to me. That's how it works. You gotta take it home. It needs you, you need it, an' I need you both back here next summer. No question about it."

"But, Samuel . . ."

"Are you talkin' back to me?" Samuel asked. "Hush now. The resonator is yours. There's no givin' it back. Fingers would be truly happy."

Samuel opened his arms and pulled me deep into his embrace. I sank into his warmth and held back tears.

"Samuel, I'm going to miss you like crazy," I told him, my voice muffled by his thick shirt.

"Me too, son," he said. "But that's good for the soul, an' good for your music. We'll be in touch other ways, you know. I know how to dial a telephone, an' I can even send an e-mail. How 'bout that?"

"E-mail? Really? Great," I said, lifting up my face. "I can e-mail you pictures and music and all sorts of stuff."

"Yup," he said, looking satisfied. "We'll be together one way or another."

Relaxing on the couch, Samuel and I talked and played long into the night. I could have stayed up until morning with him, but Jason finally came for us sometime after midnight and scolded Samuel for not being in bed. Samuel didn't say so, but he was happy about the earthquake. He loved being around kids, and he had no intention of going back to his apartment until the end of camp. Jason didn't argue. He understood his dad.

I understood Samuel too. And he, me.

Who would have guessed that I would go to music camp in San Francisco and meet an eighty-seven-year-old former Alcatraz prisoner? And more, that he'd become my inspiration and my close friend?

I wouldn't have guessed. My dad certainly wouldn't have.

But that's what happened.

And I found a one-of-a-kind teacher.

Eric's Guide to San Francisco

I think San Francisco will always be one of my favorite places in the world. When I was out there, I couldn't get enough of the trees, the bay water, and the surrounding hills. Just looking out at the Golden Gate Bridge made me feel wide-open and free.

Juan kept his promise, and during the second half of camp he took Lashley and me on tree-finding missions. My Grandpa John loved the photo album I made for him of all the different trees in the city and surrounding areas. Juan also took us across the bay and up into the Marin Headlands for a long hike. The view of the Pacific Ocean was incredible.

In San Francisco, there's just no end to things to do—neighborhoods to explore, museums to visit, parks to run in, music to hear, or foods to eat. If you plan on going, or if you just like to travel through the Internet, check out the Web sites listed throughout this guide. You can start by going to **www.sfguide.com** or **www.bayarea.com**, or by contacting the San Francisco Visitor Information Center, 900 Market Street, San Francisco, CA 94102; ☎415/391-2000; **www.caohwy.com/s/sanfranc.htm.**

Note: Entrance fees, hours of operation, and telephone numbers of the following sites are subject to change. Call for updates before you visit.

① Alcatraz Island

Visiting the cell house on Alcatraz Island was one of the most eye-opening experiences I've ever had anywhere. As soon as you get off the ferry, park rangers begin telling you dramatic tales. After you climb the steep road and put on your headphones for the 35-minute audio tour of the cell house, get ready for an intense feeling. There is definitely some kind of vibe that rattles you as you peer inside jail cells and hear the harsh sounds and unsettling memories of former inmates and guards of Alcatraz. Inspect the cells of famous gangster Al Capone and inmate Robert Stroud. Step into the solitary confinement cells called "The Hole," and see if you don't run out before someone shuts you into total darkness.

Lashley and I were lucky that a park ranger happened to ask about 20 visitors if we wanted to see the upstairs hospital unit. On our private tour, we saw where inmates underwent surgeries, where they took sitz baths, and where they were locked up if they were slipping into insanity.

The two bookstores on the island are filled with fascinating books and brochures on the history of Alcatraz Island. Look for information about the 1969–71 occupation of the defunct prison by the Indians of All Tribes. Native American activists used Alcatraz Island for 19 months as a place from which to publicize the United States' mistreatment of native tribes.

The museum is operated by the National Park Service. Ferry service is provided by the Blue & Gold Fleet. Advance purchase of ferry tickets is recommended. Ferries fill up fast, and the fleet service turns away hundreds of visitors each day.

Blue & Gold Fleet: Pier 41 at Fisherman's Wharf. Ferries leave in winter daily 9:30 a.m.-2:15 p.m.; in summer daily 9:30 a.m.-4:15 p.m. Admission includes ferry ride and audio tour. ☎415/773-1188. www.blueandgoldfleet.com or www.nps.gov/alcatraz/.

② The Cable Car Museum

This is a small but interesting museum right around the corner from Jason's apartment on Jackson Avenue. When you first enter, you hear heavy mechanical groaning underneath your feet. If you look down, you'll see the grinding of cables in the powerhouse for the city's cable car transportation system. You'll also see where the cars are repaired and stored. The exhibit shows the first cable cars of 1873 and tells about the 600 cars and the 100 miles of cable car track that were used in the city before the 1906 earthquake. Today almost 40 cable cars are in use along 3 lines. Most of the time these cable cars are packed with tourists as they are hauled up the steep hills by huge motorized pulleys. The bookstore has great souvenirs and good books on the history of San Francisco.

1201 Mason Street. April-September, open daily 10 a.m.-6 p.m.; October-March, 10 a.m.-5 p.m. Admission is free. Donations are appreciated. ☎415/474-1887. www.cablecarmuseum.org.

③ Chinatown

If you like fragrant alleys, crowded streets, and open markets, you're going to love Chinatown. It's packed with 80,000 residents–most of whom are Chinese, Vietnamese, Thai, Filipino, or Korean–and hundreds of shops and restaurants. Coming from Union Square, you walk through an archway that has dragons on it. You almost feel as if you've traveled to Asia because the streetlights, building fronts, and specialty shops all have a Chinese look. And practically everyone is Asian, except for the tourists in the souvenir shops and the business crowd in lunch places. Lashley and I went to Chinatown the first time with Jason and the other campers in our group. Since that night was cut short, we went back another time during the day. I bought all sorts of cheap Chinese trinkets for my family and friends at home.

Check out the Wok Shop at 718 Grant Avenue for chopsticks and Chinese cooking utensils, and the Old Shanghai at 645 Grant Avenue for Chinese pajamas, slippers, and silk robes with embroidered dragons. For a look at vegetable markets, bakeries, spice stores, and dumpling restaurants, wander down the less crowded Stockton Street, or the two-block area called Waverly Place.

www.caohwy.com/s/sfchinat.htm.

④ The Exploratorium

Housed within the renovated structures of the **Palace of Fine Arts**, the Exploratorium is a great science museum. With over 650 exhibits–most of them hands on–you can spend hours peering through microscopes, experimenting with magnets, playing games with electricity, and learning the physics of pendulums. The sound exhibits were the most cool for Lashley, Juan, and me.

3601 Lyon Street. Open in summer daily 10 a.m.-6 p.m., Wednesday until 9 p.m.; rest of the year Tuesday-Sunday

10 a.m.-5 p.m., Wednesday until 9 p.m. Closed holidays. Admission is charged except on the first Wednesday of every month. ☎415/ 397-5673. www.exploratorium.edu.

⑤ Fisherman's Wharf

Although the wharf–right on San Francisco Bay–can be really tacky and touristy, Lashley and I spent a whole afternoon looking into shop windows, buying treats to eat, and staring at the sea lions that live at **Pier 39**. If you're looking for a San Francisco cap or T-shirt, you can find them all over the wharf. And, you can certainly spend too much money on stuff you may not find anywhere else in the world–fun stuff that you don't really need. Although many kids will like UnderWater World on Pier 39 and the Ripley's Believe It or Not! Museum or the wax museum on Jefferson Street, Lashley and I were more interested in the historical museums. We walked west, away from the tourist crowds, to the wharves where real fishermen and women set up their rods. Lashley and I liked the **USS *Pampanito*** (a World War II submarine) and the **Maritime Museum** best of all. See more information on both places below.

www.caohwy.com/f/fishwhar.htm. or www.sfguide.com/sights/ neighborhoods/wharf.htm.

⑥ Fort Mason Center

This is where Lashley and I went to camp. If there is some activity you are dying to try, chances are good that the Fort Mason Center offers a course on it. You can learn printmaking, river rafting, Greek dancing, broadcasting, or screenwriting–to name just a few. The course that looked the coolest to me was the Shaolin Temple and Wudang Mountain Gung Fu exercise and meditation. Wow! Fort Mason also has several art galleries and museums, including the Mexican Museum and the African American Historical & Cultural Society, which I didn't have time to see. The Blue Bear School of Music also operates from the center. The campus always has lots of people running around or picnicking on the lawns. And the hostel is a great place to meet young travelers. Families can call the Fort Mason Foundation main office to find out about special programs for children. For a fabulous vegetarian meal, Jason and Samuel love to go to Greens, located down by the marina. Jason says asparagus has never tasted better, but the menu was too expensive for me to try it.

Fort Mason Center: On San Francisco's northern waterfront in the Golden Gate National Recreation Area between the Marina Green and the Aquatic Park. Open daily 8 a.m.-12 a.m. Closed January 1, July 4, Thanksgiving Day, December 25. Fort Mason Foundation: Landmark Building A, Fort Mason Center. Main Office open daily 9 a.m.-5 p.m. ☎415/441-3400. www.fortmason.org.

7 Fort Point National Historic Site

This is a great place to feel the military history of San Francisco, and to see the Golden Gate Bridge from below. Built between 1853 and 1861, the fort was meant to hold 126 muzzle-loading cannons and 500 soldiers. Lashley, Juan, Spencer, and I ran through the 3 floors of empty chambers and up to the roof to stand under the bridge. From underneath, it looked like a giant, red, steel spider web. I couldn't stop imagining the life of a Civil War soldier assigned to this dank and cold fort, long before the bridge was built. The day we were there, a group of volunteers dressed in Civil War clothing paraded through the interior courtyard and around a huge black cannon.

In the Golden Gate National Recreation Area, directly under the Golden Gate Bridge on the point of the Presidio. Because of construction beginning late summer 2001 and expected to continue 3 to 5 years, Fort Point will open only Friday-Sunday 10 a.m.-5 p.m. Call before visiting. Closed January 1, Thanksgiving Day, and December 25. ☎415/556-1693. www.nps.gov/fopo/. or www.geocities.com/sfphototour/ggbridge_ftpoint.html.

⑧ Golden Gate Bridge

I read in a brochure that in May 1937 construction began on one of the most amazing bridges in the world. Often hidden in fog, the Golden Gate Bridge connects San Francisco to the headlands of Marin. The 1.2-mile bridge cost $35 million to build, and during its construction 11 men died. The 2 main bridge cables contain 80,000 miles of steel wire strands, enough to encircle the equator 3 times.

Juan told me lots of people walk or ride bikes across the bridge every day, which can be scary because of the strong winds and the vibrating steel. If you drive across, you have to pay $3 on the southbound trip. We took a bus across the bridge when Juan took us hiking in the Marin hills. You could hear the wind roaring up there through the open bus window.

www.goldengate.org.

⑨ Golden Gate Park

This is the biggest and most amazing city park I have ever seen. There is so much to it that we only saw a small part. With eucalyptus and liquidambar trees, wide lawns, a merry-go-round, an arboretum, tennis courts, museums, gardens, and more, who could be bored in a park like that? We had a great thrill seeing the actor Robin Williams take his kids to the merry-go-round, and then we ran across some kind of international earth festival where Lashley and I had our handwriting analyzed. Juan and Spencer bought Indian tea and plastic bowls of curried rice and vegetables.

My favorite part of the park was the **Japanese Tea Garden**, where Lashley, Spencer, Juan, and I drank pots and pots of Japanese tea and ate piles of rice crackers and spiced peanuts. Standing near us was a giant statue of Buddha, which, when I looked at it, made me feel embarrassed that I had stuffed my face with food. After snacking, the four of us walked along the garden pathway across small bridges, past pools of glittering carp, and through bonsai trees. Just as Chinatown made me feel as if I had gone to China, the Japanese Tea Garden gave me the illusion that I had walked from San Francisco to Japan.

Golden Gate Park: Bordered by Fulton Street, Lincoln Way, Stanyan Street, and the Great Highway. www.goldengatepark.org (for park news).
Japanese Tea Garden: On Tea Garden Drive adjacent to the DeYoung Museum. Open daily March–November 8:30 a.m.–6 p.m.; November–February 8:30 a.m.–5 p.m. Admission is charged before 5 p.m. except for first and last hours. ☎415/752-4227 and 415/752-1171. www.holymtn.com/garden/Gallery/index_teagarden.html.

⑩ Grace Cathedral

Whether or not you worship in a church, you can still appreciate the beauty of Grace Cathedral. Stop to look at the bronze doors that are replicas of the Ghiberti doors of the cathedral in Florence, Italy. The stained-glass windows inside the cathedral are also fantastic. Because I didn't get to stay that long on my first visit, Samuel, Lashley, and I went back up to the cathedral–it's near Jason's apartment–and spent almost 2 hours looking around and sitting quietly in both the indoor and the outdoor labyrinths.

1100 California Street. Open Sunday-Friday 7 a.m.-6 p.m., Saturday 8 a.m.-6 p.m. Hours may vary during special events. Donations welcomed. ☎415/749-6300 or 415/749-6356. www.GraceCathedral.org.

⑪ Haight-Ashbury

Of course Lashley, Juan, and I had to wander through Haight-Ashbury–"the Haight"– because the neighborhood is still a symbol of rock 'n' roll music in America. Once the center of 1960s counterculture and music, Haight-Ashbury is now a place for boutique shopping or hanging out. Warning: you can't get down the street without stepping over or around drugged-out kids and pumped-up skateboarders. If you're into music, you've got to check out Amoeba Music at 1855 Haight Street, a huge store where you can buy, sell, or trade CDs, records, tapes, videos, and posters. And Juan showed us the Haight Ashbury Music Center at 1540 Haight Street, where he plans on buying a new electric guitar as soon as he has saved up enough money.

Slightly east of Golden Gate Park. To get the feel of the neighborhood, walk down Haight Street between Fillmore and Stanyan Streets. www.bayarea.com/category/california/bay_area_neighborhoods/san_francisco_city_and_county/haight_ashbury/; or go to www.bayarea.com and search on Haight-Ashbury.

(12) Japanese Tea Garden

See **Golden Gate Park.**

(13) Lombard Street

Known as the "crookedest street in the world," one block of Lombard Street is a favorite spot for San Francisco tourists. Although the residents in the area are not happy about the flood of people zigzagging down the steep incline on foot or in cars, they do not stop the flow. Because Lashley and I had both seen this famous street in movies, we had to go down it one day when we walked all the way from Fort Mason to Chinatown. Now that was a good hike.

The "crookedest" block is between Hyde and Leavenworth Streets.

(14) Maritime Museum

After wandering around **Pier 39**, Lashley and I made our way west to the San Francisco Maritime National Historical Park, where we spent a long time in this museum. My favorite part was the top room with the Morse code machines and recordings of sea wanderers' stories. There are also photo exhibits of shipwrecks and other historic marine scenes and displays of wooden figureheads from ancient ships. Designed to look like a modernistic ship, the museum has giant windows that let you look out at the bay and pretend you are at sea.

At the foot of Polk Street, near Fisherman's Wharf. Open daily 10 a.m.-5 p.m. Closed January 1, Thanksgiving Day, and December 25. ☎415/561-7100. www.maritime.org.

(15) Palace of Fine Arts

I thought that I was going to see a palace when Juan took us here, but the name is misleading. The Palace of Fine Arts is really a leftover open-air structure that was created for the Panama-Pacific International Exposition in 1915. On tall columns are carved weeping ladies that droop over you as you stand in this renovated rotunda. With nobody else around, Juan, Lashley, and I played tag between the giant columns and through the small forest of Monterey cypress trees. Not far is a swan-filled lagoon that makes you think you're not in a big city. This was a great spot for taking pictures of trees for my grandfather. The place was drenched in the perfume of eucalyptus trees.

At the intersection of Baker and Beach Streets.

(16) Pier 39

For free entertainment, go and watch the sea lions that live at Pier 39. Lashley and I must have spent more than an hour just watching them bark and swim. When you've had enough, continue through the Pier 39 shopping complex. There is a small carousel for young children, and several levels of shops and restaurants, including an international toy store. Two other attractions we didn't visit are the TurboRide, which is a simulated thrill ride, and Namco's Cyber Station Arcade, which has videogames, pinball machines, and bumper cars.

At the eastern end of Fisherman's Wharf, on the waterfront at the Embarcadero and Beach Street. Hours for shops, restaurants, and attractions vary throughout the year; check the Web site or call for details. ☎415/705-5500 and 415/981-PIER (-7437). www.pier39.com. For information about the sea lions and the Marine Mammal Center, call ☎415/289-7325.

(17) San Francisco Zoo

Even though this zoo isn't as open aired and spacious as the New Orleans zoo, it was still a great place to see animals I've never found anywhere else. The snow leopards with their thick gray fur with black spots were mesmerizing. One stared at me for minutes until I was kind of spooked and looked away. The koalas were my next favorite–fun to watch as they ate their 2 pounds of eucalyptus leaves. The zoo has all of the animals you would expect–elephants, lions, hippos, and giraffes–and others that you might not, like penguins. There's a lot of building going on, with new exhibit designs, so this zoo might become one of the most modern and innovative in the future.

Sloat Boulevard at 45th Avenue. Open 365 days a year 10 a.m.-5 p.m. Admission is charged. ☎415/753-7080. www.sfzoo.org.

(18) Schoenberg Guitars

One night Jason's camp group went to a concert at Eric Schoenberg Guitars across the bay in Tiburon. We heard the amazing Terry Robb, one of the best blues players of the

Pacific Northwest. Just being in the store was a thrill for me. Juan was right when he told me that Schoenberg's carries an awesome collection of the finest acoustic guitars ever made. They had resonator, classical, and steel string guitars, along with mandolins and banjos. I even saw a National Style O resonator with its Hawaiian etchings, just like Old Samuel's guitar. I really wanted to buy it, but I'll have to save up a lot more money first. I comforted myself by buying some new strings for Old Samuel's guitar.

106 Main Street, Tiburon. ☎415/789-0846. www.om28.com.

⑲ USS *Pampanito:* SS 383

The USS *Pampanito* is a World War II fleet submarine that operated off the coast of Japan during the war. Having never been in a submarine before, I begged Lashley to check this out with me. Descending into the cold steel vessel, I felt almost as claustrophobic as I did looking into the cells of Alcatraz prison. But, the submarine was still cool. Climbing through the narrow corridors from one cramped space to the next, I really admired the bravery of sailors who go out to sea in submarines. My favorite room was the dining area. I tried to imagine having breakfast there morning after morning without getting the chance to look outside to see what the weather was like or to breathe fresh air.

Pier 45 on Fisherman's Wharf. From the 1st weekend in October until Memorial Day, open Sunday-Thursday 9 a.m.-6 p.m. and Friday and Saturday 9 a.m.-8 p.m. From Memorial Day until the 1st weekend in October, open daily 9 a.m-8 p.m., except Wednesday open 9 a.m.-6 p.m. Admission is charged. ☎*415/775-1943.* *www.maritime.org/pamphome.htm/.*

⑳ Zeum

You can't find a much cooler place than Zeum in San Francisco if you like new art and amazing technology. This place is part of the Yerba Buena Gardens, a park right in the center of urban business. In the hi-tech classroom, they have over 20 iMacs that you can use to try illustration, video editing, 3-D modeling, and even Web site design. Lashley and I started to build ourselves a musical Web page, but we got so distracted by all the things we wanted to add to the site that we had to leave before we finished. Juan showed us the Production Lab, where one of his brothers, Jorge, hangs out every weekend and has made a multimedia show with all sorts of digital imagery and sound. You can also try drawing a character and then animating it in the animation studio. If I lived in San Francisco, I'd go back there all the time to make a music video. This place you have to see.

221 Fourth Street. Open Saturday and Sunday 11a.m.-5 p.m. Admission is charged. ☎*415/777-2800.* *www.zeum.org.*

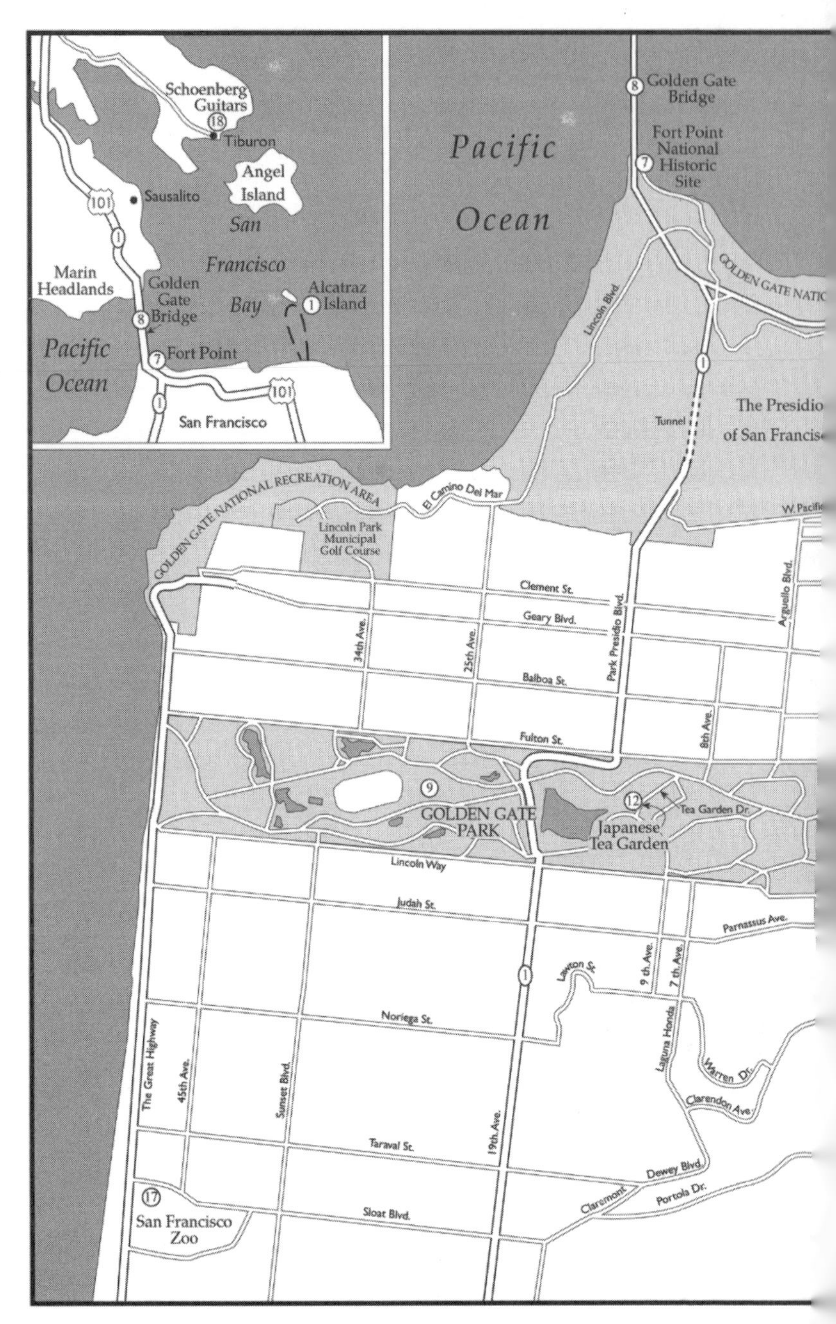
Schoenberg Guitars
18
Tiburon
Angel Island
Sausalito
101
1
San Francisco Bay
Marin Headlands
Golden Gate Bridge
8
Alcatraz Island
1
Pacific Ocean
7
Fort Point
101
1
San Francisco
8
Golden Gate Bridge
Pacific Ocean
7
Fort Point National Historic Site
GOLDEN GATE NATIONAL RECREATION AREA
Lincoln Blvd.
1
The Presidio of San Francis
Tunnel
El Camino Del Mar
W. Pacific
Lincoln Park Municipal Golf Course
Clement St.
Geary Blvd.
Park Presidio Blvd.
Arguello Blvd.
34th Ave.
25th Ave.
Balboa St.
8th Ave.
Fulton St.
9
GOLDEN GATE PARK
12
Tea Garden Dr.
Japanese Tea Garden
Lincoln Way
Judah St.
Parnassus Ave.
Lawton St.
9 th. Ave.
7 th. Ave.
1
Noriega St.
Laguna Honda
Warren Dr.
The Great Highway
45th Ave.
Sunset Blvd.
Clarendon Ave.
19th. Ave.
Taraval St.
Dewey Blvd.
17
Claremont
Portola Dr.
San Francisco Zoo
Sloat Blvd.